Came Home too Late

A Caleb Cove Mystery - #3

by

Mahrie G. Reid

www.mahriegreid.com

Copyright 2016 Mahrie E. Glab

All Rights Reserved

ISBN 978-0-9937022-8-0

This is a work of fiction. All of the characters, organizations and events portrayed in this novel are either products of the author's imagination or are used fictitiously.

During the creation of this story, various law enforcement people talked to me and answered questions. A big thanks to all of them. In real life, Bridgewater has its own police department and Lunenburg is home to a detachment of the Royal Canadian Mounted Police that serves the town and surrounding areas. The police officers and police department in this books are fictional. Although I've tried to be as real as possible, any errors are mine and mine alone.

Copy Editor: Ted Williams

Cover Design: Lorraine Paton

Dedication

This book would not be what it is without the support and feedback of my Challenge Writing Team. A huge thanks to Jessica L. Jackson, Swati Chavda and Sue Bergman. Thanks also to my number one Beta Reader, Jan Patzer. Ladies – you rock.

CHAPTER 1

Emily nodded to the clerk behind the post office counter, ran her gaze over the numbers and raised her key to the lock. She took a breath and relaxed her shoulders. She rarely received mail at this address. Rarely? Try once a year. *A girl can hope.*

She turned the key and hesitated. What did she expect? Loving words and thoughts? An actual gift? Only one person had this address and he wasn't given to any of those things. She opened the door.

An envelope stood on an angle in the narrow space. Her heart thudded louder. Her hand stayed frozen to the key in the lock. She blinked again. Still there. Her breath was trapped in her lungs. Her hand reached for the envelope. The key hung from the lock. She extracted the number 10 envelope. She knew it was a number 10. She used them in her business.

Quit stalling. You know who it's from.

She jerked one hand down to her side, with the envelope clamped between her fingers. The other hand, working on autopilot, closed and locked the door and dropped the key into her shoulder bag. Eyes focused straight ahead, she speed-walked out of the shop. When she blinked back to conscious thought she was seated in the car.

She shook her head and carefully pried up the flap. As she extracted the single sheet of paper, she laughed, a sound much like a snort. The old buzzard wouldn't have changed his mind about giving her the history she wanted. *Might as well expect pigs to fly.*

Closing her eyes, she focused on her current situation. She had friends, a job and her own condo.

The last of your friends is getting married in two days. Like the others, she'll create a new life with her husband. Have children. And invite poor single Emily to Christmas dinner and birthdays. And, oh joy, introduce me to suitable men.

Men she couldn't consider marrying. Her secret prohibited husband and children because she couldn't risk putting innocents in

2~ Came Home too Late

danger. But her friends had no idea of her past. She focused and held up the paper. The words scrolled across her brain.

Dear Emily, I know it's been years. But the time has come to make amends, to fix what I did. If I can. I am at the campground at Caleb's Cove, Nova Scotia. I'll stay here until after Labor Day. Please come if you are willing to see me.

Twice she read the words. Damn. She crumpled the paper under her closing fist. *Well, pigs do fly after all.*

She jerked her hand up, and stuffed the scrunched page and envelope into her shoulder bag. Moments later she accelerated out of the parking lot, her tires spewing gravel. She slapped at her blinker, yanked the steering wheel hard right and raced up the ramp to the highway.

But do I trust him?

She pounded her fist on the steering wheel.

Why after sixteen years has he changed his mind? Why now, why not before when we could have been a family?

. . . . .

Emily edged around the dance floor and regained her chair at the head table, settling in beside the grandmother of the bride. Her official job as bridesmaid was over. The wedding reception echoed with voices, laughter and background music, but lack of sleep left her inclined to just sit. Not that anyone would ask her to dance. She wrapped both hands around her glass and leaned her elbows on the table.

And that letter. I still haven't decided what to do.

The band warmed up for the first dance and people stopped visiting and cleared the floor. The bride and groom took center stage and the music started. The newlyweds swooped around the floor as one, the bride's arms wrapped possessively around her new husband's neck—a decidedly modern stance. Soon the father of the bride interrupted, his jacket off and his tie missing. In the time-honored fashion, he tapped the groom on the shoulder and took his place.

Mandy grinned at her dad, raised her arms and stepped into a formal waltz position. The band played on and Mandy lifted her chin and stiffened her back. She and her father executed show-worthy steps in a truly old-fashioned dance.

"I taught him that." Grandmother Bronton nodded in time to the beat.

Emily chuckled. She had no idea Mr. Bronton could dance like that. Or Mandy either. She turned to Mandy's grandmother. "Where did you learn?"

Grandma winked. "I was a showgirl," she said. "And a champion ballroom dancer." She tapped the table to the beat. "I miss it."

Emily watched and briefly imagined dancing with her father at her wedding. *Not going to happen.*

The groom reclaimed his bride, shook hands with his new father-in-law, and resumed dancing with his wife. They made one turn around the floor and the tune ended. The couple bowed to rousing applause.

The band increased the beat and gradually other couples drifted onto the floor. Soon the place was rocking with bass beats and guitar riffs. The crowd consumed drinks, men shed jackets and women kicked off their high heels. A set of 60's music had folks jiving and spinning. Voices added to the cacophony of sound.

If she left town, she might not return. Although they did not know her past, they knew and accepted her as she was. *Maybe that's good enough.*

The beat thudded in Emily's head, and she pressed fingertips to temples. If only she could pull out all the bobby pins and massage her scalp, she might avoid a headache. The last thing she needed tonight was a headache like the ones that had plagued her recently. Especially the two whoppers from the last two nights. The ones she'd had since that letter from her father.

"Don't you want to dance, dear?" Grandma leaned closer and put a hand on Emily's arm. "A pretty young thing like you should have the boys lining up." Her eyes twinkled. "Forgive an old woman, but don't you have a special guy?"

No. And not likely to. Emily shook her head but smiled at Grandma Bronton. She had too many secrets to enter a relationship requiring trust and truthfulness.

"I'm good." She covered the older woman's hand with her own. "Unless you'd like to dance with me. I could use a few tips."

"I appreciate the offer," Mrs. Bronton said. "But I think my walker would impede our progress."

4~ Came Home too Late

A slight touch on Emily's shoulder drew her attention. "Could I get you anything? Wine, coffee?" The waiter smiled. "They have a fancy machine in the kitchen for lattes and cappuccinos."

"A latte sounds wonderful," Emily said. She looked to her companion. "Mrs. Bronton, do you want a coffee, or wine?"

"Wine is what I want, but coffee is the order. A latte as well, please." The old woman smiled at the waiter.

The man reached to clear the used dishes. His arm extended from his sleeve, and Emily caught sight of black lines. A tattoo? Seemed like everyone had one these days. The waiter returned with their orders just as the band switched into the Rolling Stones tune, *I Can't Get No Satisfaction.*

Pain shafted Emily's left eyeball, stabbing in time with the music. *Time to go.*

The man dangled his tray by his side. "Anything else, ladies?"

"Once I've finished, I could use a taxi." Emily produced the taxi voucher she'd been issued when the limousine brought them from the church.

The man raised an eyebrow.

She laughed. "I'm a bit of a Cinderella." She sobered. "Actually, I've a headache."

He tipped his head. "That's too bad, miss. A taxi it is. We have the phone number in the kitchen." He nodded. "Enjoy your latte."

. . . . .

Lub-dub, lub-dub, lub-dub.
Crap that's loud.
Roll over. Get your ear out of your pillow. It's your pulse.

Emily rolled. The sound faded, but the pain throbbed behind her eyebrows, her tongue stuck to the roof of her mouth and her stomach roiled. *Headache!*

She opened her right eye and then the left. Her ceiling looked back at her. She ran her tongue over her lips. *Sandpaper tongue. I need water.*

She rolled again, this time pushing up and sliding her feet over the edge of the bed. The room rocked and her ears buzzed. Hands braced, she closed her eyes and added deep breathing. Moments later she risked looking. The ocean scene on the wall only shimmered momentarily. *Good. That's good.*

Her body ached. She looked down. *Why am I still wearing my dress?* The nausea exploded, and she dashed for the washroom, staggered and hit the door frame on the way. She dropped to her knees, pressed one hand against her midriff and retched.

I had one glass of wine with dinner. Why am I so sick?

She dragged the back of her hand across her mouth and, holding onto the vanity, pulled herself up. Her hands gripped the sink, and she leaned into them. *How did I get home?*

She released a hand and turned on the water. The water-gurgle sliced her headache. She leaned forward and scooped water into her mouth, swished and spit. Repeated. Twice.

Standing, she caught a glimpse of her hair in the mirror. No wonder her head hurt. She still had the elaborate arrangement held in place by some fifty bobby pins. She pulled them out, working as fast as her fumbling fingers would allow. When they were gone, she massaged her scalp, swept her hair back from her face and untangled the curls.

Stopping twice to lean on the wall, she stripped off dress, pantyhose, panties and bra. Naked, she turned toward the shower, but stopped with her hand on the tap.

Taxi. The taxi came before I finished the latte. I downed the last mouthful and headed for the door. The waiter opened the cab door. I got in, let my head drop on the headrest, and gave the driver my address.

She shook her head and the room tilted. Why can't I remember arriving home? She turned the taps, waited for hot water and twisted the shower lever. The hot water hit her chest, and she gasped. She turned, rotating until every inch of her skin glowed pink. She stood still then and tipped her head to let the water course through her hair.

The driver helped me to the door. The deadbolt was not locked. I never forget the deadbolt. Did I lock it when I came in?

She had to know. She shut off the water, pulled a towel off the rod and turban-wrapped her hair. She grabbed her robe and, pulling it on, hurried toward the front door.

The chain lock was engaged, but the door stood open the two inches the chain allowed.

She swallowed hard, pushed the door closed and twisted the deadbolt knob. With trembling fingers she locked the handset as well. *Not enough.* She pulled a chair from the kitchen and wedged it under the doorknob. *Just in case.* In case of what she didn't know, had never known. But her father had always warned her to be extra careful.

Locked in, she pushed her back against the wall and slid to the floor. Wrapping her arms around her legs, she pressed her forehead against her knees.

What the heck happened? Come on now, you're safe. Nothing has ever happened.

Her breathing leveled, and she swiped her hands over her face and stood. *Coffee. That's what I need.* She paused with her hand on the coffee can. Did she need the caffeine jolt or dry toast? She opted for toast. With bread in the toaster, she proceeded with making coffee.

The coffee aroma tickled her nose. *I'll be fine.* Still, she munched the toast, preparing her stomach for the coffee to come. She cupped her favorite mug between her hands and with the heat came calm. She rolled her shoulders and laughed. Overreacting or what?

A muffled version of *Everybody Needs a Friend* rang through the kitchen. *One of the girls.* She lunged for her purse and pulled out the phone and noted the time on the screen. *OMG it's almost noon. The gift opening is at two.*

"Sandra. What's up? I'm not late am I?"

"We have time, but Curt took Joey to McDonald's and I wasn't quite up to it." A yawn punctuated Sandra's words. The maid-of-honor must have stayed late at the dance. "Do you want me to come there? Or are you picking me up?"

Emily turned out her clutch purse as she listened. A roll of Evergreen lifesavers rolled onto the table. She sank down on the chair, her brain spiraling into the past.

Daddy, can I have an O?

Sandra's voice cut through the dream state. "Earth to Emily. Are you there?"

"Sorry. Ah. Okay. I'll pick you up. About one?"

"Sure. I need a shower to get rid of this rat's nest. See you then." Sandra clicked off.

Emily poked at the contents from the purse. A piece of orange paper slid out from under her compact and, with one finger, she pulled it toward her.

Hi there little Suzie-Q. How are you feeling this morning? Did you enjoy your latte last night? There's more to come. The sins of the father...you know what I mean. Someone has to pay.

Her breath whooshed out. The words ricocheted in her skull. Suzie-Q?

All real. My father's story. All real. Lately she'd convinced herself that it was all a dream. That she didn't really need to hide. That she had not seen stacks of cash. And then the nightmares would come back and she'd wake sweating, tears on her cheeks and her breath caught in her throat. And here was the proof of reality. Words from the past reaching into her life.

Her chest heaved. They found me. I've got to get away.

She threw open the closet and grabbed jeans and a T-shirt. She pulled her hair into a ponytail and, in the bathroom, dashed on a bit of makeup. She paused after a last flip of blush. *Who has found me? The police?* She sank down on the edge of the tub. *One of my father's cohorts? Or, worse. One of the men they stole from?*

Frozen ants marched tiny feet up her back and neck. Her nose chilled, an event that only happened when she was well and truly afraid. She cupped it with one hand. Was there a connection between her father's letter and this reminder from the past?

Her father had always cautioned her and urged her to run if in doubt. Whatever was happening, it was time for her to go. She made a sweep through the apartment, dumping out milk that would spoil, throwing into the garbage vegetables and other perishables. Ketchup and mustard would be fine. Canned goods—no problem. The bread hit the garbage bag. Satisfied that the place was rot-proof, she plugged in the alternating timers attached to the living room and bedroom lamps.

Back in her bedroom closet, she stood on the stool and pulled her go-bag off the top shelf. Ticking off items from her mental list, she added cosmetics and tooth care. The backpack already held her passports, extra cash and keys to her trailer which was stored one town over. There was even an additional license plate in another name—current and ready to use.

After the gift opening, she'd keep moving. Leave her car behind and head out with her truck and trailer. Her gut told her coming back wasn't smart. She snorted. All these years she'd followed her father's advice and kept the bag ready, had an exit strategy. She slung her backpack over her shoulder, picked up her purse and out in the hall tossed the garbage down the chute.

At the elevator she paused and looked back before stabbing the button. She shifted her pack and stepped in. *Never thought I'd ever really use it.*

. . . . .

The heat in the small living room at Mandy's parents' home had escalated with the body heat of friends and relatives. The windows had been opened and the front door propped ajar.

"Thanks, Emily." The bride wiggled her fingers at Emily and tapped the watercolor painting standing beside her. "This is great."

Emily grinned. "I saw you admire it enough times, I figured I couldn't go wrong." Laughter swept around the room.

The bride's mother pulled one last package from beside her chair and stood. Approaching the groom, she passed it to him. "Here you go, Scott. All you ever wanted to know about Mandy."

Amid hoots of laughter, he leafed through the huge book of photos and mementos chronicling Mandy's life from birth to wedding. He held up the book and displayed an eight-year-old Mandy with pigtails but without her two front teeth.

Mandy splayed her fingers over her face and shook her head. Looking up, she laughed and took the book from her husband. "Enough already. Let's eat, everyone." She stood and made her way into the dining room and the scrumptious spread of snacks.

Emily followed. She might as well eat before she set out. She found Sandra in the corner well into an argument about politics. She smiled, covering her regret. She'd miss those heated exchanges between Sandy and Rachel. They'd been at it since they had all shared an apartment back in university.

She touched each on the arm. "Hey, you two. Can't you leave politics for another time?"

"Sorry." Rachel shrugged. "You know how it is."

Emily laughed. "No kidding. Say, Rachel, can you take Sandra home? I've got to take off."

"So soon."

Emily nodded.

"No worries, I'll get her there." She hugged Emily. "See you soon, sista." Sandra added her hug. Emily turned away, swallowing the tears. She might never see them again. So much hinged on what happened when she met her father.

The storage lot closes at 6:00. She had no choice but to leave now. Cold prickles skittered along her arms. *On the road again.* This would make five times she'd run. Five times she'd hoped to find a safe haven. She suppressed a sigh. Each time she hoped it would be her last. Maybe this time, maybe if her father told her. Slipping in behind Mandy, she tapped her on the shoulder.

"Gotta go, girl. Tasks await." She hugged her. "Have a terrific honeymoon and a great life."

Emily retrieved her purse and headed out the door. She paused on the step, listened to the rising and falling of voices. She'd miss it, miss the girls. Would she be back? She had no idea. Given the past, it was unlikely. Given her heartache, she hoped against history that she would. Too many leavings. Too many lost yesterdays.

Shaking off the melancholy, she ran down the steps and headed for her car. She clicked open the locks, threw her shoulder bag on the passenger's seat and ran a sweeping gaze over the area. Nothing moved. She checked each car in turn. None had people watching her. Inside the car, she closed the door and engage the locks. Full precautions from here on in. She turned the key and put the car in gear.

And so it begins again.

CHAPTER 2

He followed her, watched her pick up a friend and held back while she parked. Once she'd entered the house with the open door, he coasted past both car and house. Quite the party going on. A multitude of cars parked in the drive and along the curb. *Weddings. What was the fuss about?*

His face twitched, an annoying tick that showed up under stress. He pressed his lips together to still it. He'd love to get out and put another reminder in the car for that chit of a girl. She might be grown up, but to his mind, she would always be The Girl. And she owed him, even if she didn't know it yet.

Too many people coming and going. Not safe. Ah well. No worries. He had time to kill. He chortled. *Kill. Not yet.* But no use hanging around, this shindig would last all afternoon.

He sped up, turned a corner and headed away. Time to grab a bite to eat. Then he'd go back to her place and wait for her. She'd love his surprise.

. . . . .

Three hours later he stood in Emily's living room, watching her parking lot through a slit in the blind. Damn party sure was lasting a long time. He strolled through her apartment yet one more time, rolled his shoulders and moved back to the living room.

Car doors slammed in the parking lot, and he moved to his post. *Damn. Not her. What the hell is taking her so long?* He opened the fridge door and peered in. No milk, no bread, no fruit or vegetables. He frowned and closed the door and checked under the sink. No garbage, no new bag in the bin. His face twitched. *Not good, not good at all.*

Damn. He scurried down the hall to the bathroom. No toothbrush or paste, no ladies makeup stuff. She had had a knapsack when she left. The twitch escalated. He kicked the rubbish bin. She'd outsmarted him. How dare she? He was smarter than her. He chuckled. He was smarter than most people.

Tissues and scrunched up paper scattered across the carpet. He kicked the paper again. Now he'd have to find another lever, another way to get even. Bobby-O. Or Dan. Whatever he went by, he had all that lovely money. The thought of getting his hands on his share had kept him sane in the lockup. It wasn't his fault his cousin had found him. Damn fool still, after all these years, wanted his money back and he'd decided to hold him responsible.

Bobby had promised to send Giselle money and to be around to give him his share when he got out. The man sank his fingers into his hair. But Giselle had paid him a visit in the jail. She told him Bobby had disappeared and she was struggling without the promised money. His wife and his daughter struggled right into the gutter. He didn't blame Becky for running with a bad crowd. Their downfall was the fault of that disappearing traitor. Without the promised money, Giselle and Becky had had few choices. But the life it gave her, killed her. And there'd been nothing he could do about it, not then.

You could have ratted on him.

Right, and they'd have taken back the money or they wouldn't have found him. No good in that.

No, his decision to wait, to be a model prisoner and then exact his revenge when he got out was the right one. He just hadn't thought, that once he was out, it would take four years to track down the back-stabbing, so-called friend.

He grinned. Fate had been on his side that time. He hadn't wanted to go back to Caleb's Cove when his cousin requested he take over the operation there. But it had been a good move. Not only was he raking in some cash from the operation, he'd found Bobby. The dumb-buddy had turned up back where they all started. He was older, thinner, paler, but it was Bobby-O even if he did call himself Dan Grady now.

His grin turned to a scowl. Not that he'd get the money now. His cousin, the one they'd stolen from, had cornered him and dragged him back into the life. He was paying back the stolen money from his share of the drug running. It would take a lifetime or close to it.

He shook off the past. He needed milk for that burn in his stomach and he needed to get on the road back to Caleb's Cove. He left the apartment, closed the door but didn't lock it. What did it matter? He had what he needed, and she obviously wasn't concerned. She wasn't coming back. Half a block away he retrieved his van and headed for the party house. The lights were on, people were still milling around in the living room. He passed the spot where her car had been earlier. It was gone.

One last time he drove past her apartment. Her car still wasn't in the parking lot. She was well and truly gone. Ah well. He drove slowly through town and up onto the highway. Time to head back to the east coast. He'd find another way to leverage his revenge.

. . . . .

Dan stopped in front of the office and canteen and eyed the new paint job. Lenya must have done it over the winter. The new brick-red suited the small A-Frame building. Other than that the campground looked pretty much the same. As usual at mid-week, there were ample vacant spots. Course, it might be the foggy, damp weather. He nodded. The site he preferred, the one up at the far end, was available. Its location at the end of the driveway and backing onto trees gave him a sense of safety.

He left the camper's motor running and entered the building. "Morning."

"Dan." Lenya's smile reached her eyes and creased her face. "Good to see you back." She came out from behind the counter and eyed him head-to-toe. "Lost some weight?"

He nodded. *Some weight? He'd shed pounds.*

She put a hand on his shoulder. "Are you okay?"

He shrugged and avoided answering.

She respected his silence. "I suppose you want the same spot?"

"That'd be great."

"Go ahead then. Come back and fill in the paper work after. How long are you staying?"

"Probably until after the Labor Day weekend, if that's okay."

"Certainly. Happy to have you." She patted his shoulder and stepped back behind the counter.

Dan nodded and left. Minutes later he maneuvered a U-turn and backed the truck and utility trailer onto the site. Extending the posts, and leveling the camper unit, took little time and effort but he was exhausted by the time he finished. He made sure everything was tight and locked and climbed into his bunk. One of these days he'd have to set up the lower bed. He lay on his back with one arm over his eyes. This was a trip of lasts. Last time to set up, and if he could get enough energy, a last bike ride around the island. And if all went well, a last visit with his daughter.

By the time he woke, the sun sat low in the sky and the fog and mist had cleared. He downed a full bottle of water and pulled his bike off the back of the utility trailer. He hadn't had a good ride in a long time. Hadn't felt up to it. But by gar, he was going to have at least this one. He mounted and, adjusting his gears on the high-end bike, pedaled down the campground. He nodded to Lenya who, taking advantage of the sun, was dead-heading flowers in front of the office.

Dan stopped at the junction of the campground lane and the paved road, and planted one foot on the ground to keep him balanced. His skills were compromised. He'd fallen into the bushes once or twice lately when his brain had functioned a half a moment too late and he'd forgotten to put his foot down.

To the left lay the hamlet of Caleb's Cove. To the right, the road circled around past the bridges. Traveling on the east side of the island, he would come to the older bridge first. It gave access to the second island. He doubted that he'd have enough energy to make the circuit over there. After that bridge, the road circled back to the west and he'd come to the new bridge. Replaced after a hurricane, it provided the link to the mainland and was the only way off the island without a boat.

He sighed. Coming here was a risk in more ways than one, and the skittishness that always accompanied him escalated. He clamped his jaw tighter and headed out to the right. Couldn't be helped. He didn't have much time and he needed to make things right.

In previous years he had enjoyed the scenery—the trees skirting the road, the houses old and new and the glimpses of ocean. This time he kept his focus on the road and on keeping his balance. The treatments had left him tipsy.

The road rolled out of the trees into a broad open area at the north tip of the island. Black water sloshed in the narrow space under the bridge. The second island sat silent and wooded on the far side of the inlet. Not that far away, but impossible to reach without a bridge.

    Dan propped the bike against the bridge railing and sat on a rock. The breeze had come up. He unbuttoned his denim jacket to let out the heat built up by biking. Water lapped and sucked, lulling him. Sea air cooled him, lifting his sparse hair back from his face. He inhaled, feeling the air moist and soft against his throat and tasting the brine from the ocean. Peace flowed over him.

    They'd put him in a meditation group where he'd learned to grasp moments like this, to relax into the peace. They'd said it was better, if he could. What they didn't know was the depth of his secrets. An extra zealous gust of wind flipped the front of his jacket, and those secrets took form and clamored and tussled in his head, seeking attention. He opened his eyes. *Not yet. Not yet.*

    Dan retrieved his bicycle and resumed his journey. The road looped around, past the bridge linking Dane's Island and Caleb's Cove to the mainland, and headed back toward the hamlet. His leg muscles quivered, and his breath came short and sharp in his chest. The hamlet with its shops and marina could wait until tomorrow. And the graveyard. The thought came and went. He made his way to the campground, locked up the bike and climbed into his camper. He reached for a can of soup, stilled his hand as his fingers grasped it.

    Will she come?

CHAPTER 3

The ringing phone jarred Harvey out of his contemplation. He turned away from the map and lunged for the receiver. "Conrad here."

"Harvey, I've some information for you." Constable Natalie Parker, part of the current drug investigation, launched straight into conversation.

"Hello to you too," Harvey said, insisting on at least the basic civilities. "Shoot." He edged around his desk and settled in his chair.

"We got an anonymous tip last and we closed down a drug outlet in Cole Harbour last night." Parker's energy carried over the line. "In the raid we picked up three underlings and pills that have a half-a-mil street value. The three men appeared scared skinny of their boss. Their spiel consisted of 'know nothing, say nothing'."

"Any cameras on that location?"

"They had them at the front door and the work area, but they turned them off during the delivery and pickup times." She cleared her throat. "A tech is reviewing the recording again."

Harvey grunted. "Did you learn *anything* useful?" He rocked back in his chair, stretching the phone cord to its limit and causing the chair to groan.

"Forensics is proceeding. Found some packaging that seems to have been exposed to salt water. Atlantic Ocean type water. Looks like they are still running the shipments ashore and transporting to the central point."

"Back to square one," Harvey said. "The Atlantic coast includes pretty much the entire perimeter of the province. Even with what we learned earlier, narrowing it to the south shore, we need some informants or some damn good luck."

"We can track the times these bozos had phone calls," Parker said. "And we pinpointed when their orders were issued. Assuming the texts are sent when the shipment is transferred, we got an estimate of distance between shipping and receiving. I'll send you everything once I get the phone logs and statements. And I'm going on vacation."

Parker didn't do vacation well and certainly not in the middle of a sting. Harvey shook his head. "What?"

She laughed. "Checking in with Gwen tonight. I'll be in the apartment above the marina café for as long as it takes. Jeff Brown is going to teach me to sail. See you around." The phone clicked in his ear.

Harvey scooted forward and flipped the phone onto the cradle. The drug investigation was moving forward slowly. Teams were tracking anyone making regular trips between south shore locations and Halifax. Delivery trucks, regular campers, folks living in one location and making regular visits to friends and family in the other. Too damn much data.

His section alone, the green area on the map, included seventeen store outlets with grocery delivery, seven campgrounds, and numerous folks traveling for family reasons. Even narrowed down to those with questionable backgrounds and connections, it was still a mountain of data. Not that it would help. Last year they'd picked up a guy – Joe-regular with money problems – who'd been hooked into transporting. People were suckers for easy money.

He stood, squeezed his shoulders together and headed back to the maps littered with colored pins. Four years ago they'd arrested a fellow on one of the Jewel Islands. His estate, with a deep water port and seclusion, was perfect for bringing in drugs. His house still stood empty, the walls and ceilings punched full of holes. The forensics team had left nothing to chance and, it couldn't be sold until the man was finally tried and hopefully convicted. Unfortunately, the wheels of justice moved darn slowly.

Maybe Parker, with the advantage of a harbor view on one side and street access on the other, would see something. And sailing the area was brilliant. Jeff Brown teaching her to sail was an ideal cover. Who knew what they'd find.

Constable Harvey Conrad turned away from the map and headed for the tea station. If Parker was headed to Caleb's Cove, there must be evidence pointing that way. Looked like he'd be taking lunch at the *Marina Café* more often.

. . . . .

Emily ran her gaze along the row of brightly colored shops and her tongue around the base of her ice cream to prevent a leak down the cone. The cool vanilla melted on her tongue. She licked her lips and sighed. Sometimes the small pleasures in life were the best. She rolled her shoulders and considered the *Marina Café* and the older two-story building that anchored the row of shops. Over the years, waiting for the other proverbial shoe to drop, she'd learned to make the most of each moment.

The museum, what appeared to be the oldest building in the row, sported a placard.

Shipwrecks, rum runners and family trees.
Trace the history for 400 years.
Learn the secret curse and how the cove got its name.
They must get a few tourists in the area.
Right up my alley, if I wasn't here for a showdown.

She tipped her head against the heated metal of her truck and closed her eyes. Sun beat down on her, warming her head until sweat sheeted her scalp. August. One day before her fake birthday. The wind gusted, carrying salt and cool air from the ocean. She snorted and opened her eyes.

Her real birth date was months ago. At least what she thought was her real one. Given the lies over the years, she no longer had surety in any of the details. Anger roiled through her like a flood in a coulee. Duplicity cloaked every aspect of her life. He'd taught her that. Insisted on it. And damn him, it was his history that made it necessary.

A young man came out of the café. He raised a hand in her direction. "Good night, Miss," he said, "see you around."

See you around? Why would he say that? She'd only met him over the purchase of her ice cream. She looked over her shoulder. Only one other car in the parking lot. She counted in her head. Three, maybe four had gone by on the road. She titled her head. The faint crunch of the boy's footsteps punctuated the water lapping on the pier beyond the building. The clatter of dishes echoed from the café itself.

No crowds. Uneasiness chased prickles over her skin. What the hell was he thinking? Had he become complacent, broken his own rules? She pushed away from the truck and strode to the garbage can, crushing the napkin around the tail end of her cone. She fired the mess into the can and turned away. Sixteen years of hiding in plain sight. Sixteen years with no parents, few friends, no acknowledged history. Enough was enough. She wanted more.

Seated behind the wheel, she started the engine and paused long enough to put down the windows before edging forward. The small trailer rocked over the lip between gravel and pavement. She gave it a glance and picked up speed headed for the turn-off to the campground.

She flexed her hands on the wheel. This time she would ask the hard questions. This time she'd force him to answer. Then she'd decide what to do. A vision of two older women laughing together flashed in front of her. She'd done a job for them. Helped them catalog six decades of shared history and the families behind it. They knew each other's husbands and kids, shared each other's secrets. They had each other's backs.

No one has my back.

Heaviness contracted in her chest and tears crowded the back of her throat. She wanted a real BFF, a buddy, someone who knew everything about her. Of course she'd had good times, but they were superficial, the fun of the moment only. She lived in an emotional vacuum and it sucked. She knew who she'd been from five to fifteen, but nothing before that. And it turned out even those ten years had been lies. She'd created her own world in the years since age fifteen. And now that too was compromised. She slapped the steering wheel. This time she'd get the answers even if it killed him.

. . . . .

Dan jerked out of sleep. He hadn't planned to sleep again but had been unable to stay awake. Heat in the small camper pressed down making breathing difficult. He rolled, slid down out of the bunk and hung there, his hands gripping the edge. His legs quivered, barely holding him but he managed to make it to the sink where he leaned forward, supporting much of his upper body on the counter. His tongue stuck to his teeth, and his lips brushed dry over each other.

Water, I need water.

Steeling to move, he turned and reached for the fridge door, opened it and extracted a bottle. He twisted the cap feeling the ridges bite into his skin and cursed the force needed to open it. Voices reached him and a door slammed. More campers arriving. Had she arrived? If she was even coming. He'd have to have a look. As soon as he felt up to it. He chugged most of the water and as his muscles stabilized, he took the two steps to the door and opened it.

Cool air swirled into the camper from the gray night outside. The ever-present tiredness was getting worse. He'd slept longer than he'd thought. He paused, reached into the cabinet beside him and pulled out the pills. He downed two with the last of the water and tossed the empty bottle into the bin with the others. He'd have to buy water soon. But that store. The shock of what he'd seen had nearly undone him. Lily was dead. The papers had reported it. But the woman stocking the shelves, he'd swear it was her. *The drugs are addling my brain.*

He'd backed off. Cursing the memories that had him seeing things that weren't there. They'd gotten much worse lately. He'd left without more water, still shaken even though he knew his mind was playing tricks on him. And the visit to the graveyard confirmed it. There was her stone, small, gray and sporting only her name, dates and "Beloved Daughter." What happened to wife and mother?

One foot down, the next foot placed beside it, one tread at a time he navigated the three metal steps and pulled the door closed. He leaned against the truck and scanned the campground. A couple of fires pointed out newly occupied sites. Laughter rose on the night air. Trucks poked out of parking spots along the right. Cars lined the road.

Shivering in the evening dampness, he shuffled toward the far end, checking each site as he passed. He was almost past the tidy, white unit before his brain registered the stuffed frog perched in the window. *She still has it.* Almost thirty years. Parked second from the end, her unit backed on a dense bush separating the campground from the beach. Only the trailer sat there. No vehicle. The next site, the last one, was vacant and he could see the path to the beach.

He moved on, walked along the graveled path through the gap and surveyed the curved stretch of sand. Several moving shadows revealed walkers enjoying an evening stroll. Two kids skipped stones. He watched until his stomach insisted he add food to the pills. Even though their effect sublimated the pain, they caused other problems. He turned away. He'd come back later. About to step out of the shelter of the trees, he felt the frizzed-crawl up his neck, the feeling of being watched. He paused. Listened, smelled and peered. A twig snapped off to his left. Leaves rustled in the breeze. Nothing moved in the shadows. *Imagination again.*

Dan shuffled back to his unit. He'd eat, unearth the documents; get them ready for her. Soon she could make whatever choice she wanted. One more person to meet and then he could give her everything she needed. He coughed, held his aching gut.

Time is running out.

. . . . .

Emily gave up her troubled sleep and checked the outside. Bright sun, chirping birds and roaring surf cheered the day. Wind whipped the trees and chased a bit of paper down the lane. She grabbed her gear and headed for the shower rooms. Damp, fresh air washed over her and she rounded the office. In front of her a man, with one hand against the shower building wall, coughed continuously. She kept an eye on him as she hurried forward. When he slumped bodily against the wall, she dropped her gear and reached to help him.

"Sir, what's wrong?"

The man shook his head and mouth-breathed.

Emily looked around and spied a bench. "Come on," she said "let's get you seated."

The man nodded and shuffled forward under her supporting arm. He huffed as he plopped onto the bench and tipped his head back, eyes closed.

Emily got a good look and froze. Gaunt, pale and tired looking didn't completely erase who he was.

"Dad?" Her voice cracked on the single word. "What the hell?"

The man opened his eyes, his gaze focused on her face. A half smile tipped his lips. "You came."

Her knees weak, Emily sank onto the bench beside him.

"Dad." The word whispered and, tossed by the wind, disappeared into silence. She took his hand in hers. He gripped it and there they sat. Silent. Twelve years and a lifetime of lies between them.

Was this why he'd decided to make amends? Was he so ill he was dying and looking for some kind of redemption? Is this why he sent for her? Why hadn't he written sooner? *He's my father, the only family I have. I could have helped him.*

Part of her ached to hug him, to go back to the days before her new life. Back to being a happy teenager who adored her father. The other part of her hated his secrecy.

"You're sick," she said. "Are you dying?"

He sighed, pulled his hand away and leaned forward on his knees. "Yes, to both questions."

A man came around the corner of the building, shot a glance in their direction. "Everything okay here?"

She eyed his floral shirt and the camera around his neck. *Tourist.* "Fine, just bloody fine," Emily muttered.

Dan, his face hidden below the brim of his baseball cap, said nothing. His shoulders curled and the outline of bones was visible though the layers of T-shirt and jacket.

The man hesitated and moved on. He glanced back once just before walking out of sight.

"I need to get back to my camper." Dan's hoarse voice grated on her ears. He pushed to his feet, swayed and put one hand on her shoulder. "I might need some help."

Emily stood. What else could she do? Besides, they could talk more privately away from curious eyes. She locked her arm with his and stepped forward. "Which way?"

He raised his free hand, pointing along the camp lane. "At the end," he said and emitted a coughing laugh. "I'm Dan the Bike Man."

"A bike repair man?" He'd always done office work before. "When did you take up fixing bikes?"

"Awhile back. Great cover. Lets me move around without much question."

He had a point. He probably didn't do it for the money. Piles of bills popped into her memory. After all, he had millions stashed somewhere. Surely he couldn't have spent it all in a dozen years.

They reached his campsite and he fished out a key and unlocked the door.

"If you give me a hand up the steps," he said without looking at her, "I'll manage after that. You can go for now."

"Like hell I'll go," she said.

He paused then, one hand on the door. Turning slowly, he looked her in the eyes.

She raised one shoulder. "You are a complete doorknob, but you are my father." Emily jutted her chin. "Besides, you owe me some answers."

He slumped against the door frame. "I'll give them to you later. I don't have everything ready."

Emily clamped her lips closed and shoved aside her impatience. "Come on, in you go."

He didn't argue, and she supported him up the two steps and into the narrow camper.

"Here, lie down." She helped him get settled on the couch and, grabbing a blanket off a chair-back, shook it out and covered him.

Sitting beside him, she tucked the blanket around his shoulders. Her heart rolled over. *He's so frail.* Her voice softer, she asked, "Does that last thing matter? Can't you tell me now?"

Dan jutted his chin, and she chuckled inside. She'd been accused of that move more than once. *Family traits. At least I know where that one comes from.*

Strength returned to his voice, and his tone left no room for argument. "It matters to me. Your safety is at risk if I don't sort things out. One of the others got out of jail a few years back. I need to find out where he is. I have a friend looking into it." He coughed, his hand pressed against his middle. "I'll come to your trailer later tonight, after I've called for the information. I'll give you everything you need then."

Emily pushed a stray strand of hair off his forehead and stood, looking down at his thinness and pallor.

He placed one arm over his eyes, effectively dismissing her.

She waited until his breathing shallowed, and he was asleep. Only then did she examine the space around her. *Still tidy after all these years.*

Dare she search? She looked back at Dan. His arm had settled on his chest. Not much point. He was the king of hiding things. After all, he'd hidden nearly a million in cash for years and no one had located it.

At the door, she paused for one more look, locked the handset and left him to his sleep. Striding down the campsite, she acknowledged the worry and the frisson of frustration picking at her. She still didn't fully believe he'd tell her.

. . . . .

He crouched behind the bushes. A clear line of sight let him see that mongrel's campsite. He hated the man. He should have ratted him out years ago and taken a chance on the cops picking him up... But by the time he realized the man had done the dirty and run out on him, it was too late. The trickster had a new name, a new job, a new town. There was no guarantee that the law would have been able to track him. Too bad. If they had, that little chit of a daughter would have ended up in social services. That would have been good.

So he'd kept his mouth shut. Served his time as a model prisoner, planned his revenge and got out early. Tracking the man now using the name, Dan Grady, had taken four bloody years. Years as prisoner had had an upside. He'd acquired skills that now came in useful. They didn't call the joint Crime 101 for nothing.

He shifted, braced his back against a tree and waited. He'd finally found him. The stupid oaf had come back to where they started. But then again, so had he. But he'd been forced to come and oversee the operation. It was no longer about what was left of the several million dollars they liberated back in the day. It was about paying his debt to his cousin and being his own man again.

Revenge was a different matter. Giselle struggled without the money she was supposed to get every month. A struggle that wore her down until she'd run off with a man who promised to take care of her. And he'd been locked up without a way to stop it. His so called partner-in-crime had promised to keep her safe. He'd promised to send cash-money regularly. But he'd taken HIS precious daughter and run, hiding from everyone.

But the hiding was over. And the plans were in place to extract payment.

He tilted his head to get a better look at the woman helping Dan to his trailer. It wasn't hard to see they were arguing. The woman turned and the light slanted across her face. His gut lurched, and he stood, rustling the bushes.

Lily? He got a grip and resumed his hiding spot. *No. No. Can't be. Too young.* Of course, it was the daughter. Here in Caleb's Cove, live and in the flesh. He'd seen Ms. Emily Martin up close and friendly-like back in Ontario, but with that big hair and the pink dress she hadn't looked like her mother. Now, without makeup and with her hair in a ponytail, the resemblance was uncanny.

He chuckled, remembering. He'd served her a latte drugged with just enough punch to confuse her brain. And he'd slipped those minty white circular candies into her purse. He sneered. Bet that had made her skittish. Never mind the note. And he meant what he said. The sins of the father would be paid for. If not by the father, then by the child. But they were both here. He'd hit the jackpot.

Ms. Suzie-Q you are about to lose your mind.

Too perfect. Now he'd make the lying, cheating deserter suffer. And the daughter, by the time he finished with her, she'd be unraveled. She might or might not commit suicide like Becky. He blamed his daughter's death on that coward too. Didn't matter. He'd make sure that Suzie or Emily or whoever she was, died horribly. He had useful memories and tricks to go with them. The kind that could disrupt her sleep and have her looking over her shoulder.

A thrill rolled through him. For the first time in years excitement pooled in his belly. He stayed crouched and picked his way through the woods to the beach. He had a meeting planned with the lying coward tomorrow. And everything was ready.

This was going to be fun.

CHAPTER 4

In her trailer, Emily plunked down on the sofa under the end window and reached for her frog. Hugged against her, it squished into folds and hung over her arm. What did he have to do at this stage? She plumped up the frog and stuck it back on the windowsill. A whole day to wait. Not long when she considered the fifteen-plus years since the big event. And ten before that when she had not known any differently. But until now she'd accepted she would never know, had convinced herself that life was just fine as Emily Martin. She sighed. If he'd raised her hopes and didn't plan to follow through, she might just kill him.

   She stood, stretched and her stomach rumbled. *I need breakfast*. And she'd left her towel and toiletries over by the wash shed. Time to clean up, pull herself together and make a plan. A plan to work off the energy tearing along her nerves. A plan to make the day pass faster. Action helped. That much she'd learned over the years. She headed for the door. Probably the reason she'd succeeded at everything she'd tried.

   Outside, she raised her face to the warming sun and inhaled the fresh sea air. A quick clean up and she'd get her bike. A ride would clear her head and dissipate the energy. Morning ministrations over, she stowed her gear, downed two power bars and drank a slug of milk out of the carton. In minutes she'd unhooked the bike and fastened on a knapsack. Taking a running start she headed out. At the camp entrance she hesitated only moments and turned away from town. The maps showed a road circling the island. Looked like just the right distance to burn off energy and calm her raging thoughts.

   Trees crowded the road, but here and there, squares of cleared land sported buildings and allowed glimpses of the ocean. Her breath rasped in her throat and her muscles ached. The houses spoke of families with history, people who knew their lineage. How she'd love to fill the great empty white board of her history with families. To have a house that was home, held grandparents and family memories. *Tomorrow. Hang on until tomorrow and he'll tell me.* Her foot slipped off a pedal. *But will they accept me if I find them?*

Sweat sheened her skin by the time the road rolled out of the trees and into a broad open area. The tip of the island. The bridge was older, more weathered than the one to the mainland. Stopping at the approach, she closed her eyes and recalled the map she'd picked up at the tourist bureau. There were five islands. The first three were joined by bridges like beads on a crooked necklace, and were accessible by road. Others had only boat access, islands that splayed like tossed boulders in the rolling Atlantic Ocean.

Emily propped the bike against the bridge support and slid down the scree to a rocky beach. Sun warmed her. Marvelous. She stretched out on a flat rock. Gradually peace washed over her and in spite of the sun her sweat cooled. A vehicle passed on the road above her. She turned her head and caught a flash of a floral shirt. The tourist exploring? Minutes ticked by and the world faded to dreams. The power bars wore off and her stomach rumbled once again, dragging her back from the precipice of sleep.

A second vehicle clattered over the bridge, coming from the second island, and stopped. Prickles skittered over her shoulders, and Emily opened her eyes. Who was there? The rattle of disturbed scree alerted her to the person's approach. She surged to her feet and turned, sliding one foot back, widening her stance. Just in case.

A young man slid to a halt a few feet away. *The ice cream guy. No danger.* Her muscles relaxed.

"Hey." He smiled. "Are you okay?"

Emily nodded. "Just taking in some sun."

He matched her nod. "Okay. It's just that when I saw you lying there, I thought maybe... you know."

"Thanks," she said, "for stopping. Folks around here sure are helpful."

He shrugged. "Guess so." He looked over his shoulder. "I've got my truck. Do you want a ride? I can put your bike in the back."

Her stomach again announced its need for food. "Are you headed to Caleb Cove?"

"Uh hum. But we call it Caleb's Cove." He turned and led the way up the slope. "The map makers got it wrong."

Emily moved to help him load the bike, but he picked it up and in one fluid motion lifted it into the truck bed. Seriously strong kid.

"Let's go," he said and headed for the driver's door.

"Hart," he said as he started the truck.

Heart? What about a heart? "Pardon?"

"My name. It's Hart, well, Hartlan but no one calls me that. Hart Harris."

"Emily Martin." *And I'm a fraud. Suzie Wilson at one time. Suzie somebody else before that.*

"You on vacation?"

"Sort of."

He shot her a glance.

"Collecting a bit of information. I'm a genealogist." She added the caveat before he could question what information.

"If you want family tree stuff, you'll love Uncle Lem's museum. He has a huge room with family history, pictures and stories. Everything about the island and the people. Some of it goes back to the 1700s. I thought you looked familiar, you know, in a family resemblance sort of way. Is your family from around here?"

Emily's heart thrummed. A local history. It might hold clues as to why Dan brought her to this particular location. Would the one photo she had of her mother be enough to recognize her?

"Awesome. I'll check it out." Even she heard the catch in her voice. He didn't push it that she hadn't answered his last question.

"So what's this about Caleb's Cove?" she asked.

"The place is named after a kid who was killed by thieves back in the day," Hart said. "So they called it his cove. Map makers didn't pay attention. Makes for conversation." He shot her a grin. "If you want the full story, take in one of Uncle Lem's tours. He explains it all, along with the ghost dory and other things."

She nodded and looked down the access to the mainland bridge. "Do you live on the other island?"

"No, not many folks live here year-round. I'm at university but I work here in the summer."

She laughed. "You serve up the ice cream."

"Only now and then. Redd, he's fifteen, he does the ice cream usually. I work for the EMS and for the Caleb's Cove Security Company."

"Here?"

"Yup. It's a small place but we have all the frills."

He pulled into the café parking lot. "Here you go." He hopped out and off-loaded her bike as easily as he'd loaded it. "Have their brunch special. You won't regret it." And with a wave he was gone, pulling out of the lot and continuing south down the island.

Look familiar, family resemblance.

Emily slung her backpack over one shoulder and headed for the café. Probably nothing. She had that blond-haired, brown-eyed look of thousands of other women her age. A quick glance and she could be mistaken for any number of them.

But he's had more than a quick glance. He's seen you close up twice now. She shook her head and tamped down the zing tingling her chest. *No speculation. Wait for tonight.*

Emily felt a lot better after a full meal. Hart was right. The brunch special was great. And the waitress, Kim, proved as friendly as Hart, who was apparently her stepbrother. And the owner, Gwen, had come over to say hello and turned out to be Lenya's daughter. Seemed like everyone in this place was related to someone else from the community. The concept was foreign to Emily. But she liked it.

She got on her bike and headed south down the road to The Cove Grocery Store. A few supplies and some comfort food seemed in order. Anyway, she had to pass the time until the late night. The store, situated in a three-story wood-frame building, appeared to hold just about anything she might need. From rubber boots to plaid shirts, the goods spread to canned goods, cooler items and snacks. There was even a bakery with fresh baked cheese sticks.

Emily grabbed a basket and started her rounds. Her mind roiled with thoughts of Dan, his illness, the information he was finally going to share with her. Would he tell her what he'd done that put them on the run? Give her those details? How bad could it be? Police, fellow criminals and the mob were all after him as far as she knew. That was bad. Really bad. She rounded the last aisle and headed for the checkout.

"Hey, how you doing?" The clerk sported a big smile and pink-streaked hair. "Did you find everything you need?" She watched Emily unload her stash.

"Whoa girl. Either you are having a girl's movie night or you've had one heck of a bad day. Or maybe PMS."

Emily blinked and focused on her items. Chocolate, dark and

milk, three bags of chips, two containers of dip and one honking large bucket of caramel-streaked, pecan ice cream. No bread, no milk, no hot dogs. The three items she'd planned to buy.

"Crap. I can't even carry all that in my knapsack never mind the eating." She looked up at the young clerk. "Ah. I think I need to try again. I'll put this back." She placed most of the chocolate, all of the chips and the ice cream back in her basket.

The girl laughed. "We've all had days like that. What happened?"

"Argued with my father." Emily pressed her lips together. She had not seen that coming. The works had bubbled into the world all on their own. Sharing wasn't her usual style.

"Been there, girlfriend." The clerk rolled her eyes. "It'll pass. At least my fights with Dad do." She laughed. "You should have heard him when I came home with this." She put up a hand and fluffed her hair."

"Tammy, don't bother the customers."

Emily looked toward the voice. An older woman, with a metal half-crutch encasing one arm, stood near the produce. The door beside her stood open, revealing an office chair.

"Get back to work."

"Sorry, Marta," Tammy said and waved at the woman. "Come on," she said to Emily, "I'll put this stuff back. You go get what you need." She rolled her eyes as she rounded the counter.

Emily laughed and headed for the milk cooler. She needed to adopt a carefree attitude similar to Tammy's.

Noli sinere nothos te opprimere. Don't let the bastards grind you down. She'd heard that saying somewhere. Quite appropriate.

. . . . .

Dan hunched in his hoodie, the package clutched against his belly under the jacket. He ducked behind the campsites and slipped among the trees headed for Emily's trailer. The wind was picking up and it cut through his sweats. Good thing he'd put a windbreaker on top or he'd be freezing. The moon flashed briefly and a dark shape off the side set his heart racing. He blinked, looked and saw only a stunted evergreen. He moved again. *Almost there*.

He stopped and checked. There was still a light in her unit.

Good, she'd answer quickly. He shuffled forward, glimpsed that shape again, and fear flashed through him. A stalker. He could feel it, feel the angry energy reaching for him. He hunched low, jogged past Emily's door and ducked around the tongue end of the trailer.

For a few minutes, he'd be out of sight. Time enough to hide the package with Emily's documents and the answers she wanted. He opened the flap on the side of the trailer and stuffed the package in with climbing gear, hoses and rubber boots. He pushed it up, jamming it tightly against the top where it was out of sight. He'd retrieve it for her later. Clicking the door shut, he scuttled across the vacant site and onto the beach path. Once there, he sauntered, tucking his hands into his pockets and looking up at the clouds. At the end of the gravel, he paused on the small slope. No one approached him. Maybe he had imagined being watched. He'd circle around and get back to the camper and contact Emily later.

He turned. The clouds shifted. Moonlight lit up a face. Fear shot through Dan. He hadn't seen those eyes in almost three decades. Greed had lit the eyes back then. Now the dead level stare unnerved Dan. Jail had turned the skinny boy into a well-muscled man.

And that well-muscled man looked ready to kill. No doubt he figured Dan had been living high on the proceeds. After all, several million dollars had never been recovered. Two people had died trying to get the money. One had gone to jail, and one had got away.

"Bobby-O. In the flesh. We need to talk, don't we, boy-o?" Deep and guttural the voice carried an implication more sinister than the words. A strong hand gripped Dan's upper arm and shook him. He pulled his hands out of his pockets to protect himself. *Oh crap. I'm in for it now.*

The name from his former life reverberated in his head. Dan twisted, pulled back. "Let me go." The man tightened his grip.

"Where is it?"

"Where is what?"

"Don't get funny. You damn well know what."

"What makes you think I have it? Look at my truck, my trailer. I fix bikes for money. Would I do that if I had it?"

"Bullshit. You have to have it. I been trying to find you. You don't have a Social Insurance Number, you don't collect pensions. Fixing bikes won't pay for squat." He laughed. "You don't know how happy I was to see you in the spring. Bringing that little boy a bike. Chatting up those teens. You should have stayed away." He pointed at Dan's pockets. "Turn them out. Let's see what you have on you."

Dan obliged. But all that came out of his pockets was the camper key. He resisted looking down. Where had he lost his wallet?

"Now move it. Back to your camper." The big man pulled a knife. Flipped open the blade. "Unless you want to join that daughter of yours in her trailer."

Dan shivered. But it wasn't the rain. How had this thug figured out about Emily?

I've put her in danger. He tried a bluster play. "What are you talking about? My daughter went off on her own years ago. Won't have anything to do with her old dad." His laugh, thin and reedy, carried no conviction even to his ears.

"Yeah, sure Bobby-O. And I'd like to buy Park Place. She's the spittin' image of her mother."

Dan's shoulders slumped. He should never have had Emily come here. He should have just sent the information. But he'd wanted to see her one more time before he died.

A roar of wind slashed the trees. Mist turned to rain and sheets of water raced before the wind that tossed and pushed the leafy canopy. The deluge drenched his hair and soaked into his clothing.

Voices sucked in behind the wind. A horde of kids raced up the beach toward the access path.

The attacker swore. "Get going."

Dan moved ahead of the shove.

The kids paused on the path, arguing over who had the truck keys. Dan stumbled. Out on the path, the kids hustled toward their vehicles. Dan shot a look in their direction. One tall kid kicked something on the path, looked down and picked it up. *My wallet.*

"Come on, Hart. Open the truck." A girl's voice rose over the slashing rain.

The kid called Hart stuffed the wallet into his pack and ran after the others.

The attacker shook Dan's arm. "Saw that, I did."

Car doors slammed and an engine started.

"No worries Bobby-O. I'll get your wallet back."

CHAPTER 5

Emily stood at the soup-bowl-sized sink in her trailer and spit out toothpaste. What was he up to? His truck was gone when she'd returned from her ride. She tackled the small sink, scrubbing and wiping at invisible spots. She tidied the small trailer, stacked already stacked items and refolded towels and blankets. She opened the lid on her laptop, hovered her finger over the on-button and slapped the lid down instead. She was in no mood tonight to research or write about someone else's family tree.

She turned out the single light and curled her legs under her on the bench by the back window. Moonlight revealed the road, but trees bordered every campsite, casting shadows that dipped and wavered in the off-ocean breeze. The partially open window let in the roar and suck of waves. Small rocks rattled as they rolled under the stroke of salt water. But that might be her imagination.

A shifting shape drew her attention. She leaned to the window and scanned where she'd seen the motion. *Nothing.* Down the center road she saw the shadow by Dan's camper. *The truck. He's back.* The knot in her middle eased. But would he keep his promise and come to see her tonight?

A group of teens clattered by, heading from the parking lot along the path to the beach. They lugged coolers and joked and laughed as they went. Party time. She'd never gone to parties like that and the regret mingled with other regrets of things not done. She'd told him once, way back, that she missed out on a lot of normal teen stuff because of the life he'd forced her into. He'd hugged her and said he was sorry. It hadn't helped.

She paced the short trailer, and grabbing up the book she'd been trying to read, crawled into bed. *And now he says he'll tell me the truth?* She turned on her reading lamp. Her stomach flip-flopped. The answers might set her life on-ear one more time. Could it be worse than not knowing? No answer came out of the windswept world around her. Tonight would answer her questions. Wouldn't it?

Later, she jolted awake and found the light still on and the book on the floor. Had she heard a knock? She glanced at the clock. Just after midnight. The wind howled and the trailer rocked. Branches clattered in the woods behind the trailer. A few minutes later rain pattered on the roof and she relaxed. Just a storm. The wind probably tossed a branch against the trailer.

She knelt and looked out. Dark clouds scudded across the sky, playing hide and seek with the moon. But other than a bit of paper swirling in the wind and rain sheeting the landscape, she saw nothing.

Voices floated on the wind, and she tilted her head. Which direction did they come from? Moments later, laughter joined the increasingly louder voices.

"Run guys, or we'll be soaked."

"Did you put out the fire?"

"Kicked lots of sand on it. This rain will take care of anything I missed."

The girl's voice again. "Hart, open the truck."

Hart. The young man I met this afternoon.

The kids from the party down the beach were running from the storm. Wind gusted and water pelted the trailer. It sounded like they were going to get wet anyway.

Emily let the curtain drop and sat, rubbing her eyes. Had Dan knocked? Had she missed him?

The abrupt awakening had left her pulse racing and her brain on full alert. Sleep would be difficult. She padded the four steps to the tiny kitchen and pulled out the kettle. A cup of hot chocolate might help. She drank the chocolate and kept watch on the road between her and Dan's camper. *Maybe he's too sick? Maybe he fell asleep again?*

She shook off the grief attempting to bubble up. She needed to maintain a tough stance if she wanted that information from him.

. . . . .

From outside, a woman's voice penetrated Emily's dozing state. "Jake, take your little brother. Push him on the swing. I'll be there in a minute."

"I want to go alone."

"NO, take me."

The woman's shrill tones carried thinly into the trailer. "Go on, both of you."

Emily rolled over, dug her fists into gritty eyes and propped herself up. *Morning.* She glanced at the clock and groaned—only a little after 7:00 a.m.

She pulled her legs from under the sheet and propelled herself out of the bed. *Dan?* Running to the window, she craned to see up the campground. His camper perched on its legs, and his truck was still there. So why hadn't he come?

She pulled on clothing and headed out the door. *What if he's hurt?* She glanced at some stray paper on her picnic table. Garbage. Some people had no manners. Urgency drove her. The garbage could wait. Her steps crunched on the gravel and echoed in the early stillness.

"Morning." The word floated in from her right.

She swiveled her head, raised a hand in greeting to the man in the floral shirt and kept going.

Passing the truck, she hurried behind the camper and stopped. Chewing her lip, she reached up and knocked. No answer. Maybe if she rattled the door? She reached for the handle. The door gave under her touch, and she jerked back.

If it's unlocked he's here and he's up. Why isn't he answering?

She knocked again. "Dan, are you there?"

Stillness heavier than the eye of a snowstorm was her only answer. She poked the door and it creaked open. Heat and a copper odor wafted out and dissipated around her. *This is not good.* Her stomach clenched, and her heart tripped double-rate.

She inhaled and put one foot up on the step. Taking the second step, Emily grabbed the door frame and stepped into the confines of the camper. She swept her gaze over the interior. Her attention jerked to a stop at the foot of the bunk-ladder.

"Dad." Her cry caught in her throat.

She rushed forward, slipped and landed on both knees beside him. With her hands under her chin, she stared. A red pool cradled his head. His eyes stared at the ceiling. Her eyes refused to look away.

A full breath hurt her chest, and she resorted to huffing. For a long moment, she closed her eyes, gathering courage. One hand broke free of the clutch on her chest, and she put two fingers under his jaw.

The carotid, right? I need to find a pulse. No pulse. He has to have a pulse.

She tried again. *He's dead? Dead.* The words sat heavy above her and her brain refused to let them in.

One hand over her mouth, she put the other on his chest and lowered her head. Tears welled behind her eyes.

Dead. Gone. Not coming back. But he always came back. He had to come back.

Damn you, Dad, you're all I have. A gulp punctuated her crying.

Time passed. Her nose threatened to drip, and she swiped it on her sleeve. A shaky laugh broke the deadly silence. He'd always given her heck when she did that as a kid.

Orphan. I'm a bloody orphan.

Exhaling loudly, she stood and looked from Dan and his head wound to the bunk-ladder behind him. Had he fallen and hit his head? *What do I do now?*

I have to call the police. The police? Imagine me calling the police. Irony. That's what it is.

She looked around. She'd left her cell phone behind in Ontario, and doubted Dan even had one. He had always distrusted anything that could be tracked.

Just a minute. Her brain registered what her eyes were seeing. *What's going on? This place is a mess.* She scooped up a stack of papers by her feet and put them on the small table. She stared at the fridge door standing open and the stuffing bulging from slashed cushions. A drawer under the built-in sofa hung by its last half-inch. She twisted, reached over and picked it up. Empty.

Dan used to hide things under drawers. *Check the bottom.* But the bottom held nothing. About to put it down, she spied an edge of tape and ran her hand over the flat surface. Several scraps of masking tape clung to it. Enough to show where a page-sized something had been attached.

Had Dan moved whatever it was? Or had someone taken it? She looked back at Dan. The blood, the mess. Oh no. She tossed the drawer and ran for the door, hitting the ground in one jump.

Dizziness washed over her. She leaned her forehead against the side of the utility trailer and braced her arms on either side of her head. *Dan was murdered.*

. . . . .

Dave watched the bike man's camper over the edge of his mug. The young woman had disappeared into its depths and was still there. He glanced at his watch. Twenty minutes. *Wonder what they're talking about?* He downed the last sip of coffee and, without looking, found the mug a place on the table.

The door on the camper slammed open and the woman jumped to the ground. Her forward momentum carried her out of sight behind the utility trailer.

Instinct propelling him, he launched out of his camp-chair and ran. *Something is wrong.*

On the far side of the utility trailer, he found her standing with her forehead against the trailer, her arms supporting her and her breathing perceptibly stressed.

"Miss?" Dave put his fingertips against her shoulder. "Miss? What's wrong?"

She froze on one last intake of air and cautiously raised her head, turning just enough to see him. Breathing again, she sifted her gaze past him, and back to meet his.

"The man, Dan, I think he's dead. No, he is dead."

Dave watched her face. She'd been in there twenty minutes. Had she killed him? "What happened?"

She was shaking her head. "I don't know." She put her head against her arm, her shoulders heaving.

Dave patted her back twice and turned to the trailer. He stood beside the steps and looked through the opening getting a clear view of the man's body from the brightness of the skylight. "*Mon Dieu,*" he muttered.

He returned to Emily and put an arm around her shoulders. "Come on, miss. Come with me."

He led her to his campsite and seated her in his chair. She shook visibly so he retrieved a camp blanket from his unit. "There, just take it easy. I'll handle this." He draped the blanket around her and tucked it in. "Are you going to be all right?"

She nodded, sniffed and curled into the blanket.

Dave pulled out his cell phone and walked back to the edge of Dan's campsite. Using his Internet connection, he located the closest police and dialed the number.

"Bridgewater detachment. How can I be of service?"

"I need a unit in Caleb's Cove campground," he said without preamble. "There is a body here."

"I see. Where at the campground?"

"It's in a camper at the far end of the site."

"What is your name, sir?"

"Dave Lamont."

"I've notified the closest patrol car," the woman said. "They are at the café in Caleb's Cove, they should be there quickly. Please stay on the line with me."

"*Merci,*" Dave said. "Don't be worrying, I'll be here when they get here." And he hung up. Dan Grady, a man he'd spent years searching for, was dead. His body had been found by a young woman who'd arrived recently. And he'd seen that same young woman with the victim just the day before. Curious developments. Damn, if he'd found the right man only to have him end up dead, it certainly threw a spanner in the works.

C'est dommage, mais c'est la vie. He turned and trudged back to the young woman. Unfolding another chair, he sat beside her and stuck out a hand. "Call me Dave," he said.

CHAPTER 6

Emily stuck her hand out from under the blanket. "Emily," she said and snatched the hand back after the briefest of handshakes. She watched the man from under half-masted lids. *Older guy. White hair. Confident, solid, grandfather type. But those floral shirts*. A drip of humor pierced the cold reality of Dan's death.

Normality dribbled in through that hole. Her chest curled in, buckled and ached with the loss. Her mind roiled with the anger of having her last hope snatched away. Adrift. Alone. How could she stand it?

What now?

Police will come and they will ask me questions. They'll want to know who killed Dad. She couldn't help them. She knew too little about his early years and his later years. And the middle years, nothing there that might help. She looked down the center of the campground. A patrol car had arrived and was edging toward her.

"They're here," she said to Dave.

Throwing back the blanket, she straightened her spine. Time to present the normal front of a stranger who found a body. *I must not show how much this death affected me.*

Dave stood. "Stay here, I'll talk to them first." He looked down at her. "But they will want to interview you."

She nodded, and as Dave walked away, began itemizing her morning. She would tell them she came to check on him and to see if he could have a look at her bike. She had knocked. The door was unlatched. And on through the moments she reviewed her story.

If they find out who I am, that I know him, that I am related.... How long had she been in his camper? Did Dave notice? *Suspect. I could be a suspect.*

But I know I didn't do it. And I have no idea who did. Well, she could suspect that whoever had been sending her notes, might have done it. But she didn't know who that was. She didn't want to meet him face to face. That was for sure.

She drew out of her inward focus and looked across the way. Her new acquaintance, Dave-of-the-floral-shirts, was head-to-head with the officer. *What is Mr. Floral Shirt telling the police?*

. . . . .

Corporal Harvey Conrad eyed the man who met him by the last campsite. "Are you the person who reported the body?"

The man inclined his head. "Dave Lamont," he said by way of introduction.

"Did you find the body?"

"No." Mr. Lamont looked across the road. "Young lady over there found it. She is," he said, waving both hands, "shaken terribly."

"See anyone else?" Harvey stuck a toothpick in his mouth and tucked his fingers in his belt.

"Not near the camper," Lamont answered. "Others are out and around." He tipped his head indicating the rest of the campground.

"Did you enter the camper?"

Lamont shook his head. "I have the twenty-five years on the Montreal police force, I know better."

Harvey relaxed a little. "Does she know him?" he asked, shifting the toothpick from right to left.

"Not that I am knowing. But I did see her with him yesterday."

"And you don't know the man?"

"I've seen him around here. I've heard him called Mr. Grady. I've nodded to him a couple of times since he arrived four days ago, but that's it. The sign there says *Dan the Bike Man* so I'm thinking his first name was Dan. He had the malady, a sickness, and appeared weak."

"How long have you been here?"

"About three weeks."

Harvey frowned. "That's a long camping trip? You alone?"

"Yes, just me. But my hobby is photography. Lots of pictures here." Lamont threw out his hands. "And moving camp is work, *n'est-ce pas*? I am happy to stay in this place."

Harvey blew out, dislodging the toothpick. He leaned over, picked it up and tucked it in his pocket. "Can't contaminate things."

He looked toward Emily and then back at the camper door. "I'll take a look and then we'll see where we're going."

"One more thing," Lamont said. "The unit holds the appearance of being searched and none too orderly at that."

Harvey perked up, his gaze sharpening. "You think it's more than an unattended death?"

"It is possible," Dave said. "I'll be over there with the young lady, Emily, if you need me."

"Thanks," Harvey said. He headed for the camper door where his partner, Turner, stood peering inside.

"What do you think, Turner?"

His partner turned. "It might be more than just an unattended death. Looks more like, ah ..." He glanced around at the crowd gathering in the road. "Well, more, you know? But the skylight only sheds light on the body, not the rest of the camper."

Harvey sighed. "I'll call it in and get the CS unit mobilized," he said. "In the meantime, start the tape. Nice wide circle. Take in the full site and a few feet beyond."

Turner nodded and headed to the squad car.

Harvey moved behind the camper and made his calls. The units needed would be dispatched as soon as possible. Slipping his phone into his pocket, he examined the ground and picked his way toward Dave and Emily.

"Stand back, folks," he said as he passed the crowd.

"Is the old man dead?" asked a teen. "Was he murdered?"

Pausing, Harvey peered at the boy. "Why? Do you know something? See something?"

The boy blushed. "Just guessing."

"Guessing is not good when there has been a death. Time and clues will tell us many things. But for now, we'll keep the place tidy."

The boy ducked his head and took a step back.

"They probably found a drug cache," a skinny guy said. "They used to run rum here during prohibition. There's a whole spiel about it down at that little museum place. They brought it ashore in long boats and hid it for later pick-up. I heard that happens now with drugs."

"That's not our problem," grumbled a woman with two kids. "We're not drug runners." She turned away. "Anyway, it's no place for us. Come on, kids."

. . . . .

Emily, watching Dave talk to the officer, saw him point toward her. The officer turned, his gaze direct, piercing and colliding with hers. Nerves skittered along her spine. *A person who sees everything*.

Dave left the officer and returned to sit with her. He offered no information and she didn't ask.

The cop disappeared behind the camper for long minutes and, when he re-appeared, headed in her direction. His steps sure, almost jaunty, he covered the distance quickly. *Jaunty*? Where had that come from? Cops were not jaunty. They were stern, humorless men, looking to find criminals and lock them up. Was the jaunty attitude meant to hide a piercing look, to lull folks in order to trick them into talking?

The man paused briefly, spoke with the watchers. He smiled, quick and easy, and dispersed them with his words. Damn. Why did he have to look so friendly?

A moment later he stood in front of her, his bulk a shield against the prying eyes of the others.

Dave stood, nodded at the officer and strode down the campsite toward the canteen.

"Corporal Harvey Conrad," the officer said, tucking his thumbs in his belt. "I need to ask some questions."

She nodded and sat straight in the chair. *Bring it on*. Voices chattered. Birds nattered. The ocean swished and sucked. She lifted her head. Sunlight slanted up the campsite, bathing her feet. She drew in the day, letting it push out the darkness in her head, fill the void in her chest and calm the storms in her gut.

"Miss?" The voice came from in front of her. She looked up. Ah yes, the officer with the questions. The voice seemed distant although he stood one foot away. Emily let her head tip back and looked up.

"Yes."

"Let's start with your name."

Her name? She almost laughed. Which did he want? Old name, new name, birth name? *No time for silliness*. She cleared her throat. "Emily Martin."

"Do you know the man?"

She looked toward the camper. Not really, would be her preferred answer. He'd used the present tense, do. She didn't know anything current about Dan. "No." *Semantics.*

"Where are you from, Emily?"

"Northern Ontario, north of the Lakehead."

"What brings you to Caleb's Cove?"

Was he asking easy questions to lull her? She looked around, brought her gaze back to his. "I'd heard they have a museum and genealogy material," she said. "And that it was a quiet place to kick back on a vacation."

"So, you're interested in history."

"I'm a genealogist."

"Ah." Harvey reached out and picked up the chair Dave had been sitting in. He placed it in front of her and sat, almost knee to knee with her. He pulled a toothpick out of his shirt pocket and stuck it in the side of his mouth. "Tell me about this morning," he said, taking out a notebook and pen.

She realized that direct commands replaced his questions when he wanted critical information.

Still holding onto the effects of the sunlight, Emily folded her hands loosely in her lap. "Sure." What else could she do? Short of spiriting herself away, there were few options. And, although as a child she'd tried her best, she'd never mastered magic.

What mattered now was that the police were on-site. What mattered was they were questioning her because she'd found him. Her identity had been accepted as real for sixteen years. She had education, home address and a career documented for that time and school records from earlier. Even if they were fake, they worked. Her fingerprints were not on file, her reputation was solid. Nothing should shake that life. And that life had no connection to Dan Grady, an unfortunate man, dead in his camper.

"There were some kids playing outside my trailer," she said. "Their voices woke me. I got up and thought about that man. I'd found him outside the wash-house yesterday, and he was quite weak. I decided to check on him. He'd said he'd give my bike a tune-up, if he was feeling better today." She paused and stared for long moments at the camper.

Dan might have fingerprints on file. His flight from the police had kick-started her currently shrouded life. He was the one with huge secrets. But she would be much more equipped to deal with this situation if she knew those bloody secrets.

Wait a minute. If they track his fingerprints to his original name, I'll know who I am.

Drawing in a deep breath, she held it before blowing out audibly. Detail by detail she walked the officer through finding Dan. She stated everything but the tape on the bottom of the drawer. They'd find that soon enough. She ended with her flight from the camper and the thought behind it.

"What made you think he was murdered?" The officer's voice was casual. He didn't fool her.

"Just the mess, like someone had searched or there had been a fight. When I helped him in yesterday the place was tidy. Not a thing out of place."

"Do you always help strangers?"

"It seemed the right thing to do," she said.

"And you don't know him?"

Not anymore. Not for over a decade. She shook her head.

The officer ran his fingers over his mouth and pinched his chin. "Mm." He stood, towering over her. He took out the toothpick. "Stay around. I may have more questions."

She nodded. "Okay if I go to the canteen?"

"Sure, go ahead." He looked over his shoulder and acknowledged a hand-sign from his partner.

"Later." He turned as if to head back to Dan's campsite. Before moving away, he looked back at her. "What did you do to check for a pulse?"

"Two fingers, here," Emily put her fingers against her own carotid and felt her pulse, her blood still running, her heart still beating. Nausea swarmed in her bowel, flooded her stomach and threatened her gorge. "I'm going to puke."

The officer pointed to the bush behind Dave's unit. "Back there, please, don't contaminate anything else."

Emily ran.

. . . . .

Harvey watched the vehicle lumber along the central drive with

Mr. Grady's body securely stowed in the back. The driver lifted a hand as he passed, and Harvey inclined his head in return. What would the autopsy reveal? He turned back to the row of campsites. The two closest to Grady's were empty. The retired Montreal officer, Lamont, occupied the third from the end and diagonally across from Grady.

Harvey glanced over his notes. Lamont had heard voices and sounds in the wood behind him on the ocean side as the storm broke, but hadn't seen any people. He remembered hearing a slam, possibly the door to Grady's camper. That had been just after midnight. The occupants of the tented site next in the row were gone before the body was found. According to Lamont, they were young men on a biking tour of the province. Harvey would talk to them later.

He glanced across the lane to where Turner was interviewing other campers. None of them had line-of-sight to Grady's. Harvey strolled to the older trailer next to the bikers' campsite. He stood in front of the window and looked up the lane. An overhanging branch obscured the utility trailer and the back of the camper. But he could see the truck and the camper window over the cab. Two steps later he discovered that from the door very little of Grady's site was visible.

He knocked. The thin woman who'd been with the crowd answered, her hand clutching the front of her cardigan and her shoulders tight to her ears. She kept her hand on the door. The odor that wafted out with her spoke to the unmistakable use of pot. *Great. Not going to be the most reliable witness.* But he still needed to question her.

"I'd like to ask a few questions," he said. "Would you like to sit at the picnic table?"

She licked her lips, glanced behind her and looking back, nodded. "Okay." Her shoulders relaxed as she stepped out. He waited until she was seated with her feet under the table, and then straddled the far end of the same bench, facing her. He opened his pad and clicked down the nib of his pen.

"May I have your name?"

"Lydia Mason."

"Were you here, in the trailer, last night, Lydia?"

She nodded. "Mostly. I went out for a bit before dark."

"Were did you go?"

"Out along the beach. Over to the rocks and back. The boys were trying to skip stones."

"Did you see anyone?"

She looked into space, blinked and chewed her lip. "There was a couple walking down the other way. Don't know who. And, there was one of those boats that come up around your waist out on the water. The two people in it had those double paddles." She made a side-to-side rowing motion with her hands. "But I don't know them either."

A kayak, maybe from the marina.

"When you came back, did you spend time outside?"

"Um. No. It was the boys' bedtime"

"And did you hear anything after that?"

She looked down at her hands clutched on the table in front of her and shrugged. "I was pretty tired. Drifted off to sleep early." She pulled her hands off the table and tucked them into her lap. "Some rain. Maybe some stuff hitting the trailer. Not much."

She's lying or omitting. I'm sure of it. "Did you know the man, Dan Grady?" He kept his focus on her face.

Her eyelids flickered and she licked her lips. "Not really. He had a couple of small bikes in the trailer. He let the boys use them sometimes. I only talked to him to thank him. Neither of us is much for talking. Was."

Harvey nodded, made a note. "The boys. They're your sons?"

She nodded. "Adam and Kane."

"How old are they?"

"Five and nine."

Harvey noted names and ages. "Is it okay if I talk to them?"

Her head turned toward him and her gaze connected with his. She looked down. "Why would you do that?" Her voice had gone up in tone.

Yes, for sure she's not telling me everything.

"Kids sometimes see things we adults miss." He kept his tone noncommittal, level and, he hoped, reassuring.

"Just about, ah…" She turned and looked up the campground.

"That's right. Only the same questions I asked you."

A long pause preceded her words. "I suppose. If you need to." She glanced at the trailer door, and stood. "They are over at the playground." She pulled her sweater closed and didn't look at

Harvey. "You want me to get them?"

    Harvey stood. He'd really like to talk to them without her, but they were minors, he couldn't talk to them alone. *Protocol.* He closed the notebook and stuck it in his pocket. A mental sigh accompanied the action. "How about you bring them to the canteen. I'll get them a cup of hot chocolate, if it's okay with you, and we'll talk to them there." He'd have to do the best he could.

CHAPTER 7

Ten minutes later he had Adam and Kane perched on stools with hot chocolate and cookies in front of them. Lenya, prompted by Harvey in advance, was in conversation with their mother over in the corner by the vacation fliers in their display stand.

Harvey pointed to each in turn. "Adam and Kane, right?"

The little one giggled. "No, I'm Kane and he's Adam."

Harvey grinned. "Sorry, boys." He shot his chin forward. "How are the snacks?"

"Smackin' good snackin'," Kane said.

Adam rolled his eyes. "Don't mind him. He has this rhyming kick going on."

Harvey nodded. "Do you know why I want to talk to you?"

Adam looked down at his cookie. "Because Dan is dead."

"Did you know him?"

"He was nice to us, you know. Talked normal to us, not grown-up-to-kid stuff. He told us to call him Dan and he let us ride a couple of his bikes."

"Killed and stilled," said Kane. "That's what people said."

Harvey eyed the two of them. They were about the ages of two of his nephews. Truth was the only coin they accepted, and they could handle more than many adults gave them credit for.

"Yes. It seems he might have been killed. We are trying to find out who he talked to and who he hung around with. Someone might know something to help us. What do you know?"

Adam scrunched his face. "He talked to us of course. And Mrs. Lenya." He paused, visibly thinking. "Sometimes he said hello to Mr. Lamont, but I never saw them, like, standing around talking."

"He was talking to the maidy-lady from over the clover beside the trail. They were on the bench by the wash-mosh and then they were walking and talking and walking and...."

His brother cuffed him on the shoulder. "Give it up. Mr. Conrad doesn't need your silliness."

Kane pouted and hung his head. "Well, they were." A moment later, his head came up and a grin crossed his face. "And I know something Adam doesn't. I had to pee in the middle of the night and I had to come outside 'cause there's no dump station at the site and Mummy doesn't let us pee in the trailer toilet, so I had my flashlight but it was raining and I went pee in the bush, and I heard walking, you know that sound of the rocks when you step on them and then I saw Dan and I saw another man and they were crossing from the woods over to Dan's camper and then they went behind the camper and then I heard the—" he finally drew a breath "—the door close. " He stuck his tongue out at his brother. "See, smarty pants, you don't know everything."

"You are not supposed to pee in the bushes. You're supposed to go over to the washhouse. I should tell Mom on you."

Kane's mouth turned down, and he creased his forehead. "Ah, don't tell her. You know what she'll do."

Adam sighed the sigh of an old man. "Just don't do it again. If you are afraid, get me up and I'll go with you."

Kane nodded and looked at Harvey. "Is that the stuff you wanted to know?"

"Certainly is," Harvey said. "Well done. How did you know it was Dan?"

Kane curled his shoulders. "'Cause he was walking hunched, like this. He said his stomach hurt him all the time, that's why he did it."

"Did you get a look at the other man?"

Kane shook his head. "Well, I, like saw him. I could tell he was a man. And he had a hat, it went down all the way around, not like Dan's baseball cap. I have a Toronto Blue Jays hat."

"What about his jacket and his face?"

"He did have a jacket. But I didn't see his face. It was too dark. But he kind of made me think of the man Mommy talks to sometimes. At the rocks you know, when we walk before bed."

"Shush, Kane!" Adam grabbed his brother's arm.

"Ouch. Let me go." He hung his head, and Harvey could barely hear his words. "I'm not supposed to tell anyone that."

The two brothers leaned closer to each other, their faces solemn. "You won't tell Mommy I said so, will you?" Kane looked about to cry. "She'll be really cross."

Harvey looked from Kane to Adam, and Adam nodded. "Please don't tell her."

Harvey looked to where Lenya had maneuvered Lydia Mason so that her back was to them. He looked again at the obviously frightened boys.

"I won't tell, if I can help it," he said. "Other people probably saw them. I'll get someone else so she doesn't know it was you."

His gut contracted and he watched Lydia shift from foot to foot, her hands fluttering and flapping as she talked. The woman had a problem, the kind of problem that Parker needed to know about. And as much as he hated to admit it, maybe the local social services as well.

He held out his hand. "Thank you, gentlemen, you've been a big help." He shook hands with each of them and Kane giggled. "Take, shake, make," he said and jumped off the stool.

Adam followed him. "Hey Mom, can we go to the playground again?"

Lydia looked over. Shifted her gaze to Harvey and back to the boys. "Sure, kids, sure. Go ahead."

And the boys blasted out the door.

Harvey admired the boys' ability to rise above the idiocy of adults. He checked his notes. It looked like his window for Grady's death was between midnight and 7:00 a.m. He pocketed the notebook and pen and looked up as Lenya joined him.

She folded her hands on the bar. "Well?"

He shrugged. "You know I can't comment on an ongoing investigation."

She laughed. "Can't blame me for trying. After all, it's my job in Caleb's Cove to know what's going on."

"I do have a question for you," Harvey said. "What time were people up and around this morning?"

"The usual for campers. Daylight gets a lot of them going. This morning that would have been between 6:00 a.m. and 6:30. I did my walk around about 7:00 a.m. and folks were out and about."

Harvey pulled out his notebook and recorded her comments, changing the window of opportunity. Midnight to 6:00 a.m. He'd have to see what showed up in the other interviews. And he needed to confirm where Dave Lamont and Emily Martin were during those hours. A direct question about the time would make better records.

"Thanks, Lenya. See you later."

Harvey walked up the center of the campground, Kane's observations running in his head. There was nothing in their conversation to help them ID the mystery man, but at least they knew Dan had had a male visitor. Harvey found the crime scene investigator loading boxes into the back of his vehicle.

"Well, I'm done here for now," the investigator said. "I did the interior and exterior of the camper and truck. The trailer is locked. We could break in, but I'd rather have it hauled up province and do it in the garage." He jerked his head toward the vehicles. "I've put our own locks on all of it. We'll have to have them all hauled."

"What can you tell me?" Harvey asked. "Based on what you found."

The CSI closed the tailgate and leaned against it, his arms crossed. "I can tell you what we found. Observations only."

Harvey nodded.

"The victim had bled from a wound on the back of his head. Skin and blood on the metal bracket of the bunk ladder suggest he fell against it. However, given the depth of the wound it is also possible he was pushed. He had to have hit it with some force."

"You are sure it was the ladder that caused the gash?"

"Well, we never call things sure in our business. The lab will add their findings and we'll see." The man gestured to the locked boxes in the truck. "We have samples of everything. It appeared his clothes had been wet, probably rain. There were medication bottles. Part of each label was removed. No patient name. Only drug names were left. One was morphine - pretty high dosage. The other I think is a cancer med. Not sure."

"Any home address?"

"No clue. No wallet, no mail, no pictures, nada. We'll run the vehicle plates and see what we can track."

Harvey handed over the campground registration card he'd retrieved from Lenya. "All he put on here was Halifax. Not much help."

"If it's the truth, it's a start."

"Humph. So he might be Dan Grady, or not."

The tech shrugged. "Not my call."

"Fingerprints?"

"His were illegible."

"What do you mean, illegible? Everyone has fingerprints."

"The palms of his hands were sloughing off, including the skin on his fingers. No ridges."

Harvey rubbed his hand over his mouth and chin. "Well, damn."

"Cheer up. We did find other fingerprints in the unit. Two different sets. And two different hair strands that do not *appear* to be his. Maybe we can find you some suspects." He turned to leave. "Oh, and there was a drawer pulled out of the built in sofa. Looked like something about eight and a half by eleven had been taped to the bottom. One set of fingerprints came from the drawer. Might be significant, but might belong to the woman who found him. We got her prints as well for elimination."

"Thanks," Harvey said and grimaced. "I think."

The tech slapped him on the shoulder. "Always glad to be of help. See you next time."

"Nothing personal," Harvey replied. "But I rather we not meet again—at least like this."

"I hear you. Come on up sometime and we'll go for a beer. Wash away some of the gore we deal with."

Harvey watched him go and headed for his car where Turner sat making his notes. Who could have been in the camper other than the woman who found him? She'd knelt beside him and checked his pulse. Probably contaminated things. He sighed. Not going to be an easy case, he could feel it in his gut. He headed to the car. Between the vibes he got off Emily Martin, and the suspicious omissions of Lydia Mason, his gut was having a heyday.

However, he might have something Parker needed for her case. Harvey settled in the shotgun seat and picked up the phone. He paused before dialing. "Looks like we need to know where everyone was between midnight and six o'clock this morning."

Turner nodded. "Already done."

Harvey buckled his seatbelt and dialed Natalie Parker. They needed to talk.

. . . . .

Emily stepped out of her trailer and breathed in the moist morning air. She stretched. Her night had included a lot of dreaming and subsequent tossing and turning. Crunched muscles and stiff joints didn't make for a decent start to the day. *Besides, Daddy is dead.*

Her stomach caved as if the blow had been delivered by a fist. She bent, propped her hands on her knees and gasped around sudden tears. She managed the few steps to her picnic table and sat hugging herself. She rocked and a moan escaped. How had she managed to get through yesterday and hold it together?

She sat up, sniffed deeply and wiped the tears off her face. Whatever she'd done, she needed to do it again. No one knew that Dan was her father and she'd prefer to keep it that way. She swiveled on the bench and got her feet under the table. There on the tabletop was that brown paper from yesterday. Odd that it hadn't blown off. She reached for it and pulled it closer. *No wonder it's still here, it was weighted down by a rock.* But why would anyone secure scrap paper on her table?

She moved the rock, intending to crunch up the paper and put it in the garbage. Heavy lettering stopped her mid-scrunch. Instead, she smoothed it flat. Block letters marched down the exposed inner side of the paper.

So sorry, Suzie -Q, but I know who you really are.

Her gasp was involuntary, sharp and followed by an inability to breathe. She snatched her hands away from the paper, curling her fingers into closed fists. A pain started behind her left eye. *Always the left eye before my headaches.* She stared into the trees. *I can't do this.*

You're in overload. Take a minute. Count.

She waited. She got nothing else. One, two, three…. She reached thirteen before her shoulders dropped and her brain worked. And she wished it hadn't. Fear spiders hatched in her throat and crawled relentlessly throughout her body. A moan escaped and drifted around her.

This paper was on the table before I knew Dad was dead. Before any of us did.

She sucked in air. *Except the killer.*

Dad was telling the truth. There were people after him. Anguish she'd denied for over a decade swept through her. *And they found him*. She crossed her arms on the table in front of her and rested her head, too overcome to even cry. The birds chirruped and the leaves rustled. Voices played against the space around her. Emily let the grayness wrap her tight and turn off her thoughts.

A touch on her shoulder startled her. She jerked upright.

Lenya stood beside her. "You've been sitting like that for over an hour. Are you okay?"

An hour? She must have fallen asleep. *Brain fog.* "Yes." She amended her answer. "No"

What did okay look like when your father had been murdered and an unknown person was stalking you?

"I don't know. It's been a crazy time." She sat upright, pulling the note into her lap. "I was just cleaning up." Turning so her back was to Lenya, she bunched the paper.

Lenya tsked and patted her back. "You look peckish. Come on over to the canteen and I'll give you tea and cookies."

Heat and sweets. Just what she needed. "Make that coffee," she said and stood. "And I'm all yours." She ran a hand over her head. "I'll just clean up and be right there."

"Good enough." Lenya turned and headed for the canteen.

Emily went to her trailer and stuffed the offending note under her mattress. She pulled her emotions in and tied them down with firm thoughts. She'd consider the note and its source later. After a quick cleanup she locked her door and headed for the promised coffee and cookies.

Seated on a stool by the counter she savored the first sip of coffee. "Did you hear any more about Mr. Grady?" she asked and picked up a digestive cookie. Examining the sugar crystals on its top, she continued. "Do they do autopsies on a weekend?" Her voice came out sounding merely curious, and her middle relaxed.

"The news report said it would be done next week." Lenya tidied a stack of postcards.

"News report?" Damn, she should have thought to have the radio on.

"It was pretty basic." Lenya picked up her teacup. "Just that he'd been found and an investigation was underway. There is a Friend-Connect post as well," she said. "It's obviously about the body. But they didn't release any name and the photo wasn't clear. They are asking if anyone knows him. Sounds to me like they didn't find out much about him."

Emily felt a chill. Would anyone else come forward? She might be his only next of kin.

The screen door slammed, and Emily looked over her shoulder. Dave and his floral shirt stood silhouetted against the morning light.

He nodded and headed for the coffee kiosk. "Morning, ladies."

Emily turned back to Lenya but said nothing.

Dave joined them, hitched one butt cheek onto the stool beside her and kept his left foot on the floor. "Did you see the news updates?" he asked.

Lenya nodded.

"Moi, I found out things," he said, actually lowering his voice as if sharing a secret. "He paid with the cash here, right?" He looked to Lenya for confirmation. "So, I'm guessing no bank information. Not too many people use cash anymore, at least not in larger amounts. And I heard them talking. Nothing with an address in the camper. Not even a wallet."

Feeling his gaze on her, Emily shifted. She'd paid with cash as well, and her wallet revealed very little about her. *But he doesn't know that about me.* She smiled and nodded. *Keep up the pretense of an interested party.*

Dave took a long draw on his coffee. "Ah, just what a man needs in the morning." He set down the cup and slid fully onto his seat, hooking his heels on the rungs. "Wonder what they did find in his rig?" He turned his gaze from Lenya to Emily and raised one eyebrow.

Emily shrugged. *Does he know something? Why is he giving me that look?* She had no idea what there was in Dan's rig.

The two little boys who'd woken her the morning before charged into the room, and the screen door slammed behind them. Fists clutched, they slid to a stop by the candy rack.

"I want an *Oh Henry*," the littler one said.

"No, let's get that double *Twix* and we can have one piece each."

"No, I want *Oh Henry*." The little boy grabbed for his brother's fist.

"Hey there, take it easy." Lenya came out from behind the counter. "Let's see how much money you have."

The boys tucked their hands behind their back and eyed her.

"Come on, I won't steal your money." Lenya squatted to eye

level with them.

Reluctantly they held out the coins.

She took them, pushed them around on her palm and stood. "It's your lucky day," she said, "you have enough for both an *Oh Henry* and the regular *Twix*."

"Sweet!" The older boy did a fist pump.

"Thanks, Mrs. Lenya," said the little boy and reached for the *Oh Henry*. The two raced for the door and burst out into the campground.

Laughing, Lenya returned to the counter.

"Did they really have enough?" Dave asked.

Lenya dropped the coins into the cash register and raised one shoulder. Closing the drawer, she said, "They don't often get a treat."

"Is their mother that thin woman who always looks harried?"

"She's in a bad place," Lenya said and looked out the window as a rig pulled up in the front drive. "I don't think she has any home to go back to from what I can gather. Don't know what she'll do when winter comes."

"That's tough," Emily said. "Do you know…?" Her voice trailed off as a couple came into the canteen.

"Morning," said the man. "We'd like to book a week if you have space."

Lenya pulled out a registration card. "Sure thing."

Emily stood and tossed her empty cup into the garbage. She looked at the older man and woman, and shrugged behind their backs. *Lots of room, if you don't mind the odd murder.*

Dave slid off the stool and followed Emily toward the door.

"See you," Lenya called after them.

Outside, Dave lingered beside her, his gaze direct and steady. "Well, see you around. If you need to talk, I'm a good listener."

Emily shifted under the force of that gaze. Again she had the distinct impression that he was on a fishing expedition. "I think I'm doing okay. But thanks for the offer." She strolled toward her campsite, the muscles in her back bunching between her shoulder blades. Even if she wasn't doing okay, talking to a stranger wasn't on her agenda. Especially one that gave her the same willies as the police.

She stared at the picnic table, and the black letters on brown paper rolled across her memory. Goosebumps prickled her skin. *Whoever left the note knows who I am.* She glanced at Dave's retreating back. Was it him? And if so, what did he want from her? The money? Information to find the money? She couldn't help there. She had no idea.

But can I convince him of that?

It was a thought she could have done without.

She needed to get away from this place, even for a short while. She grabbed her purse, locked her trailer and headed out in the truck. She'd head into the nearest town, Bridgewater, and have lunch out plus some shopping. There was nothing else she could do at the moment.

. . . . .

He tethered the boat on the far side of the point and hopped from rock to rock to the beach side. The clouds covered the moon sporadically, allowing only brief shafts of light. Didn't matter. He'd made the trek quite frequently. He rolled his shoulders. Between supplying that skinny-mom person, Lydia, and watching Dan, his nights had been busy. But tonight was about the girl and excitement raced in his veins. He hefted his pack of wiring and speakers and crunched across the sand to the wooded area.

Following a faint path through the woods, he came out behind the girl's trailer. A quick glance told him the note on the table was gone. He settled into watch. Waiting didn't bother him, and patience was a virtue he'd acquired over the years. No more rash running in and blowing a job. If he was honest, that rushing is what had screwed them up back in the day. Not his fault though. He'd just followed the others.

The wind came up and obliged with gusts and wailing, covering the smaller sounds of his progress. Finally satisfied, he took out wires with a micro camera at one end and a transmitter at the other. A second wire had a small speaker. That one was wired with a player. Everything he needed to remind her of her past and to record her reactions. That would be the fun part.

He'd hoped to show the recordings to Dan, but fate had intervened. The word was out all over the cove that the bike man had died overnight. Ah well. He hadn't looked too good anyway. Those pills had given away his condition. He'd searched the camper and looked up the drugs on the Internet. The bike man, formerly known as Bobby-O, probably hadn't had much time left.

He eased into place behind the trailer where a bush sheltered him from the main path. Working as silently as possible, he slid under the trailer and with his hand auger, made a hole under her bed. When it punched through, he installed the speaker and wire and taped the player under the edge of the unit. Far enough in that it couldn't be easily seen and close enough for him to reach it.

The camera would be trickier. He slipped along the trailer and peered at the window that should be over the kitchen sink. He'd already checked it and seen the curtains. If he got the tiny camera positioned right and flush with the wall, it would be virtually undetectable. He was sweating by the time he got the unit installed. Backing off to the woods, he pulled out his iPad and checked. *Hot damn I'm good.* The interior of the trailer, although dark and shadowed, showed up nicely. It gave him a limited view of the entry and kitchen area. Not as much as he'd like, but better than nothing. He was ready.

Packing up his other gear, he retraced his steps, found the woman's payment under the usual rock and left her a little something to ease her day. He felt like whistling but that would not be a smart move. And he'd learned to play things smart. On the far side of the point he sat in the lee of large boulder and lit a cigarette. He blew smoke rings. Another thing he'd learned when he'd had time to do nothing else.

Wonder how she'd liked the sympathy note? That was a good one. Now what can I do for an encore? Frogs, she always liked frogs. And she has the stuffed monstrosity in her window. Yes, I'll have to do something with frogs.

CHAPTER 8

Emily stayed away until after dark. She did not want to talk to anyone connected to the campground or Dan's murder. A mug of hot chocolate and a few pages of reading in bed and she slid into sleep, her last thought a wish for no nightmares.

The music drifted in her dreams. A voice unaccompanied by instrumentals sang *Farewell to Nova Scotia.* A song she hadn't heard in years. She couldn't identify the female singer, but somehow she felt she should be able to. She rolled in the bed, punched her pillow. *It's night. Has to be a dream.* The singing stopped. *Mommy sing it again.* Emily rolled over once more, dragging the blankets with her. She slid out of the dream and back to sleep.

Pictures played in her head. She knew she was dreaming, but couldn't move a muscle, could not force her brain to wake up. A doll with yellow hair lay on a carpet and her father was yelling. Yelling at what? She tried to see but couldn't. In the dream, the little girl crept away and crawled into her secret hiding place dragging the dolly. A huge stuffed frog waited for her. It pressed down on her and she tried to push it away. Using both hands and feet, she pushed against the lid on the window box. The lid refused to move. More yelling leaked in around the girl, the doll and the frog. *Not Daddy this time*. One final swirl, and the images disintegrated.

Morning came. Dead silence cloaked the world. The silence thudded in her head and her pajamas clung to her damp skin. *The nightmare. It's back.* She struggled out of bed and the air hit her skin, chilling her. Beyond the window, the fog had settled over the landscape, masking vision and sound but adding damp salt and seaweed odor. Emily yawned, curled up by the table and tucked in her feet. Moments later, her fuzzy brain fired a memory. *That music. So familiar. So haunting.*

Who had been singing? She closed her eyes and in her mind

looked at each campsite. The older couple in the next site usually turned in early because they would be up at the crack of dawn to go birding. The next site was vacant. Then there was the mom with the two boys. Adam and Kane, she'd heard them called. Might have been their mom, but it was pretty far away for the singing to have carried through the dense trees separating one campsite from the next. Then three young men who were bicycling around the province and at the end, Dave Lamont's site. None of them seemed candidates for being the singer.

Flashes of her dreams played on her closed eyelids. Too fast to capture, too real to ignore. *I had dreams years ago. My screams would waken Dad and he'd come and comfort me. But I could never tell him what was in the dream.* She opened her eyes and, returning to the bedroom, dressed hurriedly. Heading to the wash house, she eyed the sites on that side of the road.

Across from her trailer, the office, the wash houses and the playground stretched out in a row. The next site was the couple who had arrived only the day before and then there were two sites vacant before Dan's. Maybe someone had been out for a walk. Yes, that was it. Someone taking a midnight stroll must have been singing. It had to be.

She stopped by the canteen for hot coffee and, shoulders curled against the damp, headed back to her trailer. A nice hot bowl of porridge and an egg or two and she'd feel steadier. The food did help, but the uneasiness remained and she pulled the brown paper bag with its note out from under her mattress.

Suzie-Q. It has to be someone who knew me as a toddler. Dad never called me that after Mom was gone. And Dad brought me here to the type of location he always avoided. Why? Was it because someone here knows me, knew him?

She started a pot of her own coffee and stood rubbing her fingers against her temples. She'd felt the same fogginess the day after Mandy's wedding. That time she'd been sure she was drugged. But how could that have happened here? The coffee pot beeped and she added hot coffee to the paper cup from the canteen. *Assume for the moment you are right where you need to be.*

Duh. Of course. *You could dig around. You are a genealogist.* She sat at the table with her hands warming on the cup. They even had a museum here. And people she could talk to. *I need to get out there and mingle. Listen to people. Find out the history of the place, the families who've been here a few generations. Start digging.*

Her father's words echoed in the silence. *Never look back. Never look for what happened. You are safer if you don't know.* But she'd been fifteen when he cut her loose, even though the identification he'd bought for her said she was eighteen. Surviving had taken all her energy. And moving from place to place, figuring out how to survive, had left her no time to dig into his past. She'd wondered a few times. But always, his words and the fear behind them shut down any looking.

But now, he's dead. So how can looking into his past hurt anyone? Couldn't be any worse than it already was, with him dead and a stalker watching her.

She'd start looking. But first she'd write down everything she could remember, every little snippet floating around in her head. She could dig out the two or three old photos she had hidden. If she didn't examine the pieces, how could she put the puzzle together? Wasn't that what she told her clients? That any small memory may be the key to open the door. Energized, she jumped up and put her breakfast dishes in the sink.

She ran some water on them and with her hand on the tap to shut it off, froze. One memory popped out of her subconscious. Goosebumps rose along her arms, across her neck and around her waist.

The sea-bound coast. My mother sang that song.

She turned off the tap and rested her head against the cabinet. *What is going on?*

. . . . .

She was careful where, and with whom, she consumed alcohol, but for this project the fewer inhibitions she had the better. Blocking old memories, ignoring dreams and her inner questions for over a decade had locked down her memory center. She poured a glass of wine. She needed all the help she could get to unlock that vault. *Or maybe it's false courage for what you might find.*

The real vault, hidden under the base of her kitchen sink cabinet, held only a few things. But they were all she had from her first five years with both parents, and the following ten with just her father. If she let her mind roam, maybe those mementos would trigger other memories. She pulled the drapes closed, opened the under-sink cabinet and lifted the tightly fitted floor panel. Recalling the combination, she opened the safe door and removed three black and white photos, one two-inch square jewelry box and a red leather wallet.

Once they were laid out on the table, she retrieved the stuffed frog from the end windowsill. A zippered bag to hold pajamas, its cavity was currently stuffed with a battered, yellow-haired doll. With all her mementos collected, she sat back to contemplate each item.

She started with her name. The first time her father had changed their names, he'd kept her first name as Suzie. For ten years she'd been Suzie Wilson. She'd looked up the name years ago. One of the top English names in several countries, Wilson was first recorded in 1342 in England. *Like that information is of any help. Not.*

It was only when he'd had to send her off on her own that her identity had changed to Emily Martin. She downed a slug of the wine and focused on the warmth running into her belly. *Emily Martin, Emily Martin who the hell are you?* A noise halfway between a laugh and a snort came out of her.

Paper. I need notepaper or a notebook. I need to write things down. She found the tools and started free-writing on each of the items.

Mid-afternoon she scarfed down a power bar and, putting her arms on the table, and her head on the arms, dozed, dreamed and woke to add to the list. The years from five to fifteen had some solid memories of reading dozens of books, of being on the debating team at school and running for student council. Her friends, Paula and Carol, had been left behind without a word.

And the money on the living room floor. She'd never forget that. She massaged her temples. This was hard work. And the years with her mother only came in flashes of memory.

The horror of seeing a dog squished by a truck had stuck with her as had the warmth of being curled in bed with her dolly. The other snippets were as disconnected and vague. Mommy smelled of flowers and Daddy ate macaroni and cheese with molasses on top. Emily tossed down her pencil. None of those details connected to anything concrete. It was all the emotionally charged highlights of her life. She drained the second glass of wine.

She capped the bottle and stood. She needed exercise, not more wine. Pulling her items toward her, she dumped the silver necklace out of its box. She thought it was her mother's. It might have been given to her when she was really little. Another detail she couldn't recall.

The clock read four-thirty and she glanced out the window. There was still enough light for a quick bike ride. That's what she needed. Pushing hard enough to make her muscles burn. Feeling the wind in her face. It would clear the mess in her head. She returned the items to their places and snatched her helmet from the rack by the door.

A memory flashed across her mind. Her pulse kicked up several notches, her breaths became short. The urge to pee assaulted her. She put a hand on the door frame and sucked in a deep breath. The visuals were gone, illusive. But they were the ones from her nightmares. Of that she was sure.

Her body's response could be flight or fight. It might depend on what lurked in her memory to cause it. She ran her hand over her forehead, wiping off the moisture collected there during that short dip into a flashback. *Not now. Not now.* That memory would wait. But it would be back, to tease her and frighten her, the way it had for over two decades. She opened the door and stepped away from the fear.

Outside, the still air lingered warm from the afternoon sun. People were straggling back from the dory races over at the marina. She'd forgotten about them. No wonder it had been so quiet all day. She stretched, and fastened on her helmet before heading to the bike rack. She rounded the back corner of the trailer and put out her hand. Her fingers met air where her handle bars should be. She blinked. Looked again. Her bike, usually securely locked with two locks, was gone. Stolen. *Well, damn it all anyway.*

. . . . .

Emily checked her watch. 9:00 p.m. It had taken time to search the area around the campground and to ask others if they had seen anyone with her bike. Everyone, except the boys' mother, had been at the dory races. Dave had taken the boys with him and the mom had had a nap. Now Emily was back at her campsite with the two boys in tow.

"We'll watch for it, miss," Adam said. "I know what it looks like. If we see it, we'll bring it back."

Emily resisted the urge to tousle his hair. "That'd be a big help," she said. "But be careful, if someone has it, just come and tell me."

"Okay. We can do that." Adam took Kane's hand. "Come on, Mom will be cross if we don't get to bed." He headed out with his little brother dragging behind.

Emily sighed. Lenya had insisted on calling the police. She'd said it might have something to do with the murder. At the very least, the police should have a report in case Emily wanted to file for insurance. Emily couldn't argue that one.

She took one last walk around the trailer, and retrieved the locks from the picnic table where she'd put them. They had been snapped by some type of cutter. Inside the trailer, she tossed them on the sofa. Between the memories, both remembered and elusive, and the stolen bike, her mood had sunk to a new low. She needed sleep and a fresh perspective.

Who took the bike? Should I call the insurance?

She took down the hot chocolate mix.

I'll live without a bike for now. I'll get one back home.

Two tablespoons of chocolate mix went into the cup. She added a third. She needed chocolate.

If I go back home. This is making me crazy.

She opted for warmed milk to make the chocolate and settled on the sofa to enjoy her drink. She'd barely finished it when her eyelids drooped. No way could she stay awake any longer. But once in bed, dreams plagued her. Music drifted in her head. Disembodied talking and laughing supplemented the music.

At one point her brain seemed to be awake, but her body was locked in a dream paralysis-state, and she struggled between reality and illusion. *I should wake. Something is wrong.* Aware of more music she rolled again and plunged into the familiar, deep, dark nightmare that always left her sweaty and scared. Of what she did not know.

A lighter sleep marked the arrival of sunup. Emily stirred and pulled the pillow over her head to block the light attacking her eyelids. A flicker of sheet brushed against her foot. She rolled onto to her side and pulled up her leg. Her mouth was dry and her ears buzzing. A moment later the tickle slithered over her calf. Her brain registered the movement. Emily's eyes popped open. She lifted the top blankets and peered under. Parked by her kneecaps and staring up at her was a snake.

Her scream rose and fell as she tossed the blankets, swung her feet over the edge and jumped from the bed. Her heart pounded in her chest and her breathing stuttered in her throat. More flutters and tickles assaulted her feet. She screamed again and looked down. *Frogs.*

Croaking penetrated the fog in her brain. The entire floor was covered with frogs. Her legs shook and her pulse throbbed in her throat, pounded in her ears and pressed against the top of her head. She looked around, leaned to put her hands on the table and stepped up onto the bench. She closed her eyes. Willed the floor to be bare. Looked again and held back the urge to jump out the window. Where the hell had those damn things come from? And how did they get inside past her locked door?

For a long moment she stood there with her eyes closed. Her body, weary from a night of tossing and turning, ached. Not only was her mouth dry, but her head had that foggy, buzzy thing going on. Like back home after the wedding. She opened her eyes. Had she been drugged?

She couldn't see how or when someone had drugged her. But she hadn't heard anything like someone breaking in. She couldn't stand there thinking about it. She needed to get out. She had to get to the other bench and out the door from there. The other option was to step back into the swarm of slick, cool bodies and tiny probing feet. She shuddered. A few frogs she had no trouble with. But there had to be dozens of them. One of the frogs attempted a leap onto the bench. It missed and she gave it a "so there" gesture with her hand.

To get over to the second bench was her preferred option. She got there and, bracing one hand against the wall, flipped off the locks on the door. She turned the handle and shoved—hard. It only opened about four inches before thumbing against a blockage.

Confused, she tried again and it swung free, revealing Constable Conrad nursing his knuckles.

"You didn't have to bang my hand with the door."

"Help. Me. Out of here." Her voice came out strong and high, unmistakably both shaken and demanding.

"What?" He looked down as two frogs made a break for freedom. "What the…" he took in the rest of the floor, shook his head and held up both hands. "Come on then, before your friends tackle us both."

Emily grabbed the offered lifeline and they stood, holding hands, for a long moment. *Holding hands is nice. Not getting me out of here. But nice. What is the next move?*

"Oh crap," Conrad said. He planted the left foot on the top step, his back against the door frame and, shoving frogs out of the way with the other foot, planted it on the floor. Straddling the threshold, with one foot in and one foot out, he pulled her hands up to his shoulders.

"Here, put your hands on my shoulders. I'm going grab you around the waist, and pull you toward me. Latch on like a drowning kid, and I'll get us both out of here."

Moments later, Emily had her legs around Conrad's middle, her arms clamped on his neck, and they were in a flying leap out of the trailer.

Conrad landed, took one extra step to get his balance and held her tightly against him. She was aware of his body from her thighs wrapped around his middle to her arms wound around his neck. *My goodness he's solid.*

Conrad's partner, Turner, came around the corner of the trailer. "Whoa," he said. "When did you two get so friendly?"

CHAPTER 9

Awkward. Emily dropped her legs from around Conrad and sliding her hands to his chest tried to step back. She cleared her throat. "Thanks." What else could she say? But she felt the heat in her cheeks and saw the grin on Turner's face.

Conrad let his arms drop away from her body.

Chill settled where she'd been warm for those brief seconds. She stepped back and clasped her hands in front of her. Darn P.J.s didn't have pockets.

"Where the heck did you get the frogs?" he asked.

"I didn't," Emily said. "They were here when I woke up this morning."

"They were just here?" Conrad sounded unconvinced. "Did you leave your door unlocked?"

A chill raced over her skin. She'd forgotten about that. She shuddered, even more unsettled by the thought that someone had had access to her while she was asleep than she had been by the frogs. She whirled around and headed for her door. She'd unlocked it to get out, hadn't she?

"It was locked." The mutter came out from between her clenched teeth.

"Pardon?" Conrad stepped in beside her. "What did you say?"

"I locked the damn thing," she said.

Conrad leaned over and checked the lock. "Doesn't look like it was forced."

"I don't care what it looks like. It was locked."

"Might have been picked," Conrad said. "Would have taken someone with master skills. That's an unusually heavy duty lock for a trailer."

Turner stepped in on the other side of Emily and made his own inspection of the lock. Both men kept their gazes forward, but the silence was eloquent with shared disbelief.

Emily huffed and backed away. Totally not responding was her go-to operational mode when she couldn't, or didn't want to, explain herself.

The officers turned to her. "You didn't hear anything?" Conrad asked.

Emily shivered. There had been music and voices but they were in her dreams. Why had she not heard the door? It was loud enough it should have woken her. After all, over the years she'd learned to wake quickly, easily at the slightest sound. Had the door been picked during that dream where she couldn't move? Had she been trying to respond?

"I should have." Scratchy fear colored her words. "But I didn't." The mouth dryness reminded her about the drugging option. She kept that to herself.

Conrad crossed his arms, and Turner pulled out his notebook and wrote in it.

Laughter drifted across the road, a contrast to the gloom settling around Emily. She looked to where Adam and Kane were chasing each other in a game. When was the last time she'd been that carefree?

Conrad turned and whistled. The boys stopped and looked, and when Conrad waved an arm, they came running over.

"Good morning, Mr. Conrad, not bad, not sad," Kane chanted at him.

Conrad tousled his hair. "How do you feel about frogs?" he asked.

"They're green," Kane said, "and mean, and…." Adam poked him and he stopped.

"Around here," Adam said, "you can find Pickerels and Northern Leopard frogs, especially this time of year. There's a pond over there." He waved his arm toward the top of the campground and away from the cove. "But Mom doesn't like us to go there."

"You know about frogs," Emily said.

Adam nodded. "I have a book with pictures and sometimes we catch a Northern Leopard in the fields. But the Pickerels like ponds and Mom doesn't like us to go by ourselves." He stopped, the completion that she didn't go with them hung in the air.

"This is your lucky day," Conrad said. "We have had a frog

delivery, and they are loose in Miss Emily's trailer. We need someone to catch them and take them back to a pond. You two are just what we need. Go get a big box from Lenya and I'll talk to your mom. Constable Turner will help you and go to the pond with you to let them loose."

"Yippee." The boys raced away and Conrad turned to Emily. "I'll be right back. Then we need to talk." He headed toward the boys' campsite, beckoning for Turner to follow him.

Five minutes later the boys were in her trailer under Turner's supervision. The three of them were laughing and chasing frogs. The snake had already been found and was curled in a jar, waiting for its freedom.

Emily watched from the doorway. *Hope they catch them all. I sure don't want to find one in my bed tonight.* She sighed. How had they ended up in her trailer in the first place? Was it from the same person who left her those mint candies and note after the wedding? The same weird person who had left the sympathy note?

She'd liked frogs when she was a kid, it was the reason that someone in her past had given her the plush frog. A puzzle piece of time busted out of her memory banks. She was catching a frog with a net. She'd been so excited. But who the shadowy figure behind her, helping her was, remained as elusive as her nightmares.

Excitement wasn't her mood of the moment that was for sure. She shook off the memory and turned away from the trailer.

Conrad joined her. "How are they doing?"

"They are having fun," Emily said. "And they seem to have more frogs in the box than are left on the floor."

"Good. And you have no idea where they came from?"

She shook her head. And that was the truth. She had no clue as to how, when or why the frogs had ended up in her place. Well, maybe the why. Someone wanted her to connect with her past. But to help her? Or scare her?

"Does anyone else have a key? Or have you lost a key since you've been here."

Again she shook her head. None of those parameters applied. She was damn sure to keep her keys safe. Never even put one in those under-the-wheel-well magnet cases. As far as she was concerned, that was an invitation to steal the vehicle.

"Humph." Conrad pulled a toothpick out of his shirt pocket.

"That brings us back to someone picking the lock." He stuck the pick in his mouth and gazed at the sky.

Emily stole a glance from the corner of her eye. What was he thinking? She'd be darn skeptical if she was in his place. After all, who in their right mind bothered to catch that many frogs, never mind stick them in someone's trailer?

But he was right. If there were no extra keys, then some broke in. Quickly, silently and efficiently from the way things looked. That was a truth she could have done without. If he, or she, had picked the lock once, they could do it again. Fear she thought she'd banished over the years, swooped in on her. Her safe place was no longer safe.

"Run me through what you did after you searched for the bike?"

Emily pulled out her ponytail, scooped her hair back from her face and reapplied the elastic. "I came back here, went in and," she said, glaring at him, "locked the door."

"And?"

She huffed. "I made hot chocolate…" She ran him through her routine.

"Do you always drink hot chocolate before bed?"

"Only if I have no other form of chocolate around."

"Hmm, what about your bike?" He shifted the toothpick from one side of his mouth to the other. "When did you notice it missing?"

"I came out about five or so to go for a ride."

"And the bike was locked up?"

She shot him a look. "Two locks, both cut."

"Why two locks?" He seemed mildly curious.

"Expensive bike."

He inclined his head in acknowledgment. "When did you see it last?"

"I went out two nights ago. And I locked it up when I came back."

"Okay then. Let's go have a look at the scene of the crime."

Emily pointed to the back of the trailer and followed Conrad as he headed that way.

They rounded the back corner and Emily stopped. She blinked. She couldn't be seeing correctly. Her bike hung in its stand, chains and locks firmly in place. Her head spun and her knees almost let go. Had she dreamed it? No. Lenya had called the police, and that's why

Conrad was here. She looked at him, opened her mouth.
No words came.

. . . . .

Harvey looked from the bike to Emily. What game was she playing? Reporting a bike stolen that wasn't? And finding a horde of frogs inside a locked trailer. How did he know she hadn't put them there herself?

"Well," he said. "Is this your bike? The one you reported missing?"

She stood looking at the bike, one arm clutching her middle and the other hand splayed against her throat. The look on her face could only be called stricken. Why? Because she was caught in a lie? Or for some other reason?

She nodded. "I don't understand." Her words were muttered, but he heard them. "I just don't understand. It was gone last night. The locks were cut."

"Do you have those locks?"

She whirled around and almost ran to the trailer door. He followed as she took one big step into the trailer. No frogs were in sight, and the boys had carried their catch to the picnic table. Turner was helping them tuck in the flaps to contain the frogs.

Emily ran her hands over the sofa, checked in the cracks between seat and side and along the back edge. She knelt and ran her hands along the floor in front of the sofa skirt. Sitting back on her haunches she stared at him.

"They're gone." She ran one hand over the sofa cushions again. "I put them right here." She looked out at the frog collectors. "Did you boys see any locks when you were catching the frogs?"

Adam and Turner looked over and shook their heads.

Harvey pressed his lips together but said nothing. *Is she lying? Why? What does she have to gain?*

"Come on," he said. "Come and sit outside and tell me everything you remember about last night and this morning."

She followed his bidding and sat across from him at the outside table. The boys had left, taking the box of frogs with them.

"I was busy inside all day," she said.

"Doing what?"

"Working on notes for a client."

Harvey noted a slight hitch in her speech right before the last word. He nodded.

"I had a snack and decided I needed some fresh air so I grabbed my helmet and came out to get my bike."

Harvey listened as she ran through the rest of her story. "Did Lenya come and check the bike rack?"

She shook her head.

They sat silently. What else could he ask her, other than to ask her if she was lying?

She snapped her fingers. "The boys were here. They saw the empty rack—I think."

"Good. I'll talk to them when they come back." Harvey stood. "I'd like to search your trailer, if you don't mind." It wasn't a question, only a courtesy.

Emily's eyes went wide and she raised one eyebrow. "Why?"

"In case something else was left here, not just the snake and frogs." He didn't add that now he was interested in seeing if she had the keys and wallet from Grady. And one other thing struck him. "Do you have the keys for your locks?"

"Yes." Emily stepped into the trailer, got the keys and led the way back to the bike. She fitted a key in the first lock. It worked. And the second did as well.

"Humph." Harvey took out the toothpick and stuck it in his pocket. "Now that is odd."

Emily looked at the keys and the lock. She ran her finger over the ridges on the keys. "These are sharp," she said and held them toward him. "Like they are new. Mine were old and smooth."

Harvey nodded and took the keys. They did look new, but he had only her word that they should be worn. "Okay." He handed the keys back to her. "We'll put that in the report."

And now he'd like to search and he'd like to get a sample of that hot chocolate mix. It was a slim chance, but someone might have drugged it. Someone who knew her habits. Although how someone would, Harvey didn't know. He'd have to talk to Lenya and see if Miss Emily Martin had had guests.

He felt her gaze on him and met her eyes.

Puckered mouth, frown lines and then a smile that bent her lips but did not light her face followed one on the other. A lot was going on in that head of hers.

She licked her lips. "I guess your search is next." Her words didn't carry any warmth. She was as reluctant as any suspect he'd ever interviewed.

. . . . .

Between a rock and a hard place. Maybe a cliché, but so true at the moment. Emily watched Conrad head to the trailer, pulling latex gloves out of a pocket. He snapped them on and stepped inside. It shouldn't take him long. The interior floor area in the light-weight trailer was only ten feet long and about three feet wide. Of course he'd look inside cabinets and closets as well. He was a cop.

She chewed her lip. *As long as he doesn't find the safe under the cabinet.*

With her stomach drawn into knots, she waited, tipping her head to catch any sounds from the search. Instead the crunch of gravel drew her attention.

Lenya crossed the last few feet from the road to the table and stood beside her. "What's this about frogs?" she asked.

"Woke up and found them in my trailer." Emily turned her hands, palms up, signaling she didn't know anything more. "Someone's idea of a practical joke, I guess." She smiled, attempting to make light of the moment. She did not mention the bike was back in its holder. That little detail still had her flummoxed.

Lenya sat beside Emily. "You've had a tough week. Finding Mr. Grady's body was bad enough, but the bike theft and now the frogs." She shook her head. "You need some young folk to talk to. Go over to the café. Gwen serves a mean brunch. I'll call ahead and tell them the meal is on me."

"You don't have to...."

Lenya held up a hand. "Don't have to. Want to. Gwen is my daughter. Sit and talk to her a bit. Do you good."

"But Conrad is...." Emily stopped under the force of Lenya's gaze. "I have to lock...."

"No problem, I'll make sure he locks your place and brings your keys over to the café." She stood and put a hand on Emily's shoulder. "Go on, child. You need a break from this nonsense."

Her hand was warm and firm, conveying support. As least Emily took it as support. She wasn't sure what support felt like. She opened her mouth to object again.

Lenya raised a finger and grinned at her. "Go on now. Listen to Mother." She looked toward the trailer. "I'll deal with Harvey. You just go."

That did it. The last thread of Emily's resolve snapped. Tears threatened, and she coughed into her hands to cover up. She stood and headed for the trailer. Grabbing her keys and her wallet, she headed for her truck. At the moment, it was a relief to let someone else make the decisions.

. . . . .

The man was up early. He wanted to be watching the video feed when the girl woke to find all those frogs. He flipped on his iPad. Had she liked the frogs? He snickered, cradled his coffee and settled to watch her cope with the horde. Too bad he didn't have sound. He'd bet she screamed when she found that snake.

The thrill of a sudden, remembered fear sliced him. Had she felt like that? Motion drew his attention. The look on her face was priceless, and he laughed. *Too bad, girlie.* She lifted her feet away from the frogs and climbed onto the bench. Darn, that was too short, too easy.

Flipping the lock open, she pushed the door. It bounced back. What the heck? She pushed again and the trailer door swung open. The man swore. That blasted policeman, Constable Harvey Conrad, stood there. The man gritted his teeth. If offing a policeman wouldn't attract unwanted attention, he'd happily do the man in.

Emily placed her hands in the officer's outstretched palms. They shuffled, and in moments she was wrapped around the officer, and he'd swung her onto the ground. The man threw his mug across the room and swore loudly. *Too easy. Too bloody easy.*

The two disappeared from view, and anger surged through him. She was not supposed to have any support. She was a loner. Why was she not alone? *Bloody police. Nosy do-gooders. Interfering pigs.* They always screwed things up. If they hadn't been around back in the day, things would never have come to this. They'd all be living the high-life somewhere warm.

His teeth ground harder, and he closed his eyes. *Calm down. Remember, no tension.* He drew in air and consciously relaxed his jaw. He had that high blood pressure thing going on and was supposed to avoid stress. Easy for the sanctimonious doctor to say. He didn't have illegal drugs to transport, or an old, not-so-nice friend killed before sharing the money. Or, he opened his eyes and snorted—a girl who had to die to avenge her father's sins.

He got a bowl of cereal and watched again as the two little boys and Constable Turner appeared. It had been easy to learn the names of kids and cops. All he'd had to do was have coffee at the café and listen carefully. He could see snatches of the removal crew as they chased and caught the frogs.

Damn. Looked like the little brats were having fun. Soon the girl went into her bedroom and come back in street clothing and, after that, Conrad returned and started searching. Would he find anything? Any clue to the money? Probably not. The cops were good at searching but, the man blew on his finger tips and polished his nails on his shirt, he was better.

The girl appeared in the doorway and pulled up a sliding panel on the top of the bench back. A fairly good hiding place, but he'd found it. He'd made impressions of keys and created a full set for his use. He could come and go as he pleased, and if he decided to so do, could take off with her truck.

A blur obscured his view. The cop had found the camera. *It's not fair.* Nothing of any use would come through his peek-a-boo setup now. Disgruntled, the man shut off the iPad. Would he be able to get over there and remove the recording and transmitting unit before they got their techs out there? Or would that Conrad fellow take it all away? Either way, he'd have to go and check.

CHAPTER 10

Emily stopped at the junction. The east road and the main road connecting the village with the bridge to the mainland lay before her. *Left and I'll end up in the café on display with nosy people all looking at me.* Her stomach clenched. The urge to flee propelled her thoughts – *go right.* Safety lay in the road off the island and bigger towns offering anonymity.

Decision time. *Do I run or do I engage?* Even coming to Caleb's Cove had been fueled by running from that first note and the mint candies. *I've run for decades.* She pulled in her abdomen and pressed her back against the seat. *Firm spine, girl. Time to face things head on.*

She slapped the blinker control down, made a left turn and headed into the unfamiliar. Even back home, when meeting friends she'd come to know gradually, she'd been sure to be the first one arriving at a meeting place. She liked to grab a table in a corner with a wall behind her.

In spite of her attention to safety, exercise and defense skills, she didn't take chances on anyone surprising her. Even in recent years, when she'd grown safer, she hadn't let go of the safety habits. Now, with her father murdered and someone stalking her, those habits were needed more than ever.

Inside the café, a reception counter with a back wall blocked the view of the room. Emily stepped past the counter and swept her gaze over the space. Red checkered tablecloths covered the tables and a single flower sat in the middle of the each. Both the bright colors and the enticing aromas welcomed her.

A plump, blond lady, about her own age, looked up, saw Emily and hurried toward her. "Welcome, Emily. Mom said you were on your way over."

Unexpectedly, she hugged Emily while Emily stood stiffly with her hands by her sides. She wasn't a hugger. More than that, she was not even a toucher. Body contact dented the boundaries of her personal space.

The blond stepped back. "I hear that you've had a shock or two in the last few days," she said. "Come on in and we'll get you a good meal and some friendly conversation." She led the way to a table at the back of the room. Two other women were already seated, and they looked up and smiled as Emily and Gwen approached.

Emily hesitated. One new person she could manage. Three at the same time? Not so sure.

Gwen either didn't notice her hesitation, or chose not to. She pointed. "This is Devon, and the pregnant one is Kelsey. Guys - this is Emily Martin." She added no other details, but they nodded as if they knew who Emily was.

"Sit," Devon ordered. "Gwen just brought us tea and ginger cookies. We like to eat our meals backwards." She laughed. "Sweet things first."

"Or sandwiched," Kelsey added. "We might have more dessert at the other end."

"Over here," Devon said, indicating a chair in the corner. "You'll feel safer."

How did she know that? Emily looked at her sharply, but sidled behind Kelsey to the corner chair. She sat, hung her purse under the chair back and folded her hands on the table.

What do I do now? Are they going to grill me with questions I don't want to answer?

Gwen picked up a huge, brown teapot and turning over the mug in front of Emily, poured out steaming tea. "There you go," she said. "Help yourself to the cookies. There are more where they came from." She pulled a crocheted tea cozy in red and white over the pot. "I'll be right back," she said and headed toward swinging doors at the back wall.

"How do you like your trailer?" Kelsey asked.

"Pardon?"

"Your trailer. I want to get a small trailer so I'm asking everyone who has one what they like about theirs."

"Ah. Well, it's small, but it's enough for me," Emily answered. She pointed a finger at Kelsey's middle. "Not sure it'd work with a baby on board."

Kelsey grinned and planted a hand on her rounded belly. "I hear you."

Emily dug into her memory for questions she'd heard folks ask her friend, Faith, when she was pregnant. "Is this your first? And do you know if you're having a boy or a girl?"

"Yes," Kelsey answered, "my first. And no, we didn't find out the sex yet. Sam, my husband, wanted to be surprised." She smiled that serene smile of expectant mothers.

Emily grinned. Faith had looked like that—until after the baby arrived and she'd had a few weeks of sleepless nights. Her smile had been occasionally forced after that.

Turning to Devon, Emily asked, "How about you? Have you any children?"

Devon nodded. "Grace is just turning five and Ivan is nine months. Greg is looking after them right now."

"Greg is your husband?"

"Yes."

Gwen returned and slipped into the seat across from Emily.

"And you all live here?" Emily waved her hand.

"We do now," Devon said. "But we didn't at first. Like a lot of folks still do, we only came for the summer—May long weekend to October Thanksgiving weekend."

"We used to winter in Halifax." Kelsey picked up the explanation. "But more folks are staying year round, including us."

"I've always been here year round," Gwen said. "We keep the café and gas bar open."

Okay, okay what else can I ask? It was such a small place. What could people do for work? "What other work is there here?"

Devon took a sip of tea before answering. "Our husbands," she said, flipping a finger between herself and Kelsey, "run a business from here. Their work is all over the world, so it really makes no difference where they live. Kelsey is the accountant, and I handle the bookings and disbursals and communication as needed."

"So a family business?"

"Sort of," Kelsey said, "although Greg and Sam are not related and neither are we. Around here family isn't always related by blood ties. Choice plays a big part."

Emily mulled over what she'd said. That family could be had by choice had never entered her mind. But even if it had, would she have entered into a closer relationship with her friends. *Not if it meant giving up my secrets.*

"How about you?" Gwen asked. "What's your family story?"

Damn, she'd paused too long. She hated that question although she'd had more than enough practice in answering it. "I'm an orphan and then some," she said with a laugh. "No family at all."

"Sorry," said the other three in unison.

"No worries," Emily said. "I'm used to it."

Silence took over as they munched cookies.

"How long have you known each other?" Emily asked to keep the conversation going.

Devon spoke up. "I've known Gwen since we were kids, I came here every summer to my uncle's place. We both met Kelsey about, what, three years ago now." Kelsey nodded. "She came here with Sam, who has known Greg for twenty years at least." She cradled her tea cup in both hands.

Kelsey picked up the conversation. "They were at college together and then as trainees on the Calgary Police Force."

Emily's radar went up and her imaginary bubble shield came down around her. *Cops. Damn it anyway.*

"Now they offer high-end security and discrete private investigations. They are both home right now, but in two days they're heading to Europe to do a five day security tour with a visiting ambassador."

Not much better. But probably okay as long as no one suggests they investigate me. Two servers showed up carrying steaming platters with a mix of food.

"I didn't know if you liked seafood," Gwen said. "So I had Frank prepare a mixed platter. Scallops, salmon, mussels, and chicken bites, just in case. And rice, mashed potatoes, mixed vegetables and coleslaw." The servers returned with the side dishes as Gwen finished speaking.

"Goodness," Emily said, "I may not have to eat for a week after this. I'm up for most of this, but I've never had scallops or mussels."

"Once you try them, you'll want them forever," Kelsey said, handing Emily a serving spoon. "I had never had them either, but you can't keep me away from them now."

The conversation that interspersed eating turned to babies, toddlers and books. "We read a lot here," Kelsey said. "TV shows get old pretty fast. We have book club. The three of us," she said, "and Marta from the store and her mother, Mrs. Gerber and sometimes Kim." She pointed to the young female server. "When she's home from university, that is."

"What do you read?"

"Pretty much anything. But we do have an obsession with murder mysteries." Gwen paused. "Sorry, didn't mean to bring up murder over dinner."

Emily shrugged. "No worries." And the conversation went back to Elizabeth George, and Louise Penny.

They cleaned the platters and Kim, and the other server, removed the dishes.

"Okay," Gwen said, "who's up for some blueberry grunt?"

Emily wasn't sure she had heard correctly. "Say what?"

The other three laughed, and Kelsey explained. "Don't worry, it's just stewed blueberries with sweet dumplings steamed on top. It's delicious."

"Why is it called blueberry grunt?" Emily asked.

"The berries make little popping or grunting sounds as they get hot and burst open," Gwen explained. "It's a longtime dessert here on the south shore."

"Makes a certain sense."

Chatter around them ebbed and flowed as patrons came and went. The bell over the front door clanged, announcing a new arrival. A woman with a cane that hooked around her arm came around the counter.

Gwen looked over. "There's Marta. Probably came to pick up her lunch. We try to get her to stay, but she likes to get back to the store." She waved, summoning Marta.

Moving surprisingly quickly, Marta crossed the room.

The waitress nodded to her. "I'll get your lunch."

Gwen made the introductions. When she came to Emily, Marta turned her head slightly, as if getting a different angle on what she saw.

"Of course," she said. "I've seen you in the grocery store. That's why you look familiar."

Emily nodded. "I've shopped there a few times." She met Marta's gaze. The direct look and the sparkle in her eyes belied the scar running along her hair line. Had Marta been in an accident? *Not the kind of thing to ask a stranger.*

Marta's lunch arrived, and bidding them all good-day, she left.

Devon sat forward. "We have a confession," she said. "We have another club besides the book club. It includes the three of us and a few more. And you've just met the criteria for membership."

Emily tensed. Criteria? What criteria?

"It's called the Touched by Murder Club."

Oh man, that's weird. Touched by Murder - what kind of people had a club called that?

Emily sat at the café table, her back to the wall and wondered if she had heard Devon correctly. *Touched by Murder Club.* That was a new one. She put one hand over her forehead to check her temperature. Maybe she was hallucinating. No. Forehead was fine.

"Do you want to run that by me again?" she asked.

Devon sat forward and rested her forearms on the table. "I know. It is a bit weird. But all of us have been somehow connected to a murder, and it has affected each of us differently, but not well.

"Membership comes if you find a murdered body, if you are related to someone murdered, if you are stalked by the murderer, or pretty much any type of kickback in a murder situation. We meet occasionally and have fun as a way to override terrible memories. If someone is having a flashback, they can call one of the others to come and hang out with them. That sort of thing. It helps us cope."

Emily stared at her. Cities racked up numerous murders. Maybe even towns had a few a year. But this place? "You actually have enough people, here in Caleb's Cove, to make a group about murder?"

All three women sighed and nodded.

Gwen's face took on a pinched look, and she glanced from Devon to Kelsey.

"I know. It takes a bit to wrap your mind around it. Sometimes we defer to the curse concept."

"A curse?"

"Uh hum."

"You're pulling my leg, right?"

"We don't really believe it, even if so much has happened that fits the story." Gwen tipped her head and pursed her lips. "Sometimes it's easier to believe it's a curse rather than the evil of men." She sighed.

"Okay then. Who else is in this group?" Emily looked around the room occupied by a handful of people who were probably a mix tourists and locals.

"Hart for one," Devon said.

"Hey, are you talking about me behind my back." Hart's voice came from the doors that led to the ocean front patio.

Emily looked over and there he was, heading toward them. Devon stood and greeted him with a hug. "We were just adding Emily to the *Touched by Murder Club*."

"What? What happened to Emily to deserve that?"

"Grab a chair," Kelsey said. "And we'll tell you. It's about the other night."

"Hey, I'm going to take it back to the campground as soon as I'm done here," Hart said as he retrieved a chair from an empty table.

"Take what back?" Gwen asked. "We wanted to talk to you about the man who was found dead."

"Dead?" Hart reared back. "Who's dead?"

"One of the campers. Didn't you hear?"

Hart shook his head.

"Emily found the bike man dead in his camper. Looks like he was murdered."

The young man sat, rubbed his chin with one hand. "Holy ape-shit." He shook his head several times and said it again.

Emily followed the exchange without a word. Sorrow cloaked her shoulders and soured the meal she'd just eaten. But what could she say? *He was my father*? Not a smart move until she knew a whole lot more. Until she knew who was stalking her.

"Now," Devon said, "what were you taking back to the campground?"

Hart pulled out a black, tooled-leather wallet, the edges overlap-bound with leather cord and closed with a flip and snap. Scuffs and marks revealed its age.

Dad's wallet. Emily squeaked and put her hand over her mouth.

Kelsey shot her a querying look but didn't interrupt Hart.

"This," Hart said holding it up and pulling their attention back to him. "It's the bike man's wallet. It was on the path when we were running from the rain. I kicked it the other night after the beach party. I figured he wouldn't miss it until morning." He gave a shoulder twitch. "But then Jackson hauled me off to Halifax before dawn the next morning, and we just got back now."

"The police will want that," Devon said. "You'd better give them a call."

Hart sat upright in his chair, his nostrils flaring. "Am I in trouble?"

"Did you open it?" Kelsey raised an eyebrow at him.

"Just to look at the ID. It's the emptiest wallet I've ever seen. Mr. Dan Grady only had a driver's license and an insurance card. Oh and an old, old picture."

Emily held her breath. She knew the picture. The one with her and her parents. One of the two remaining photos of the three of them. The other was back in the trailer, in her matching leather wallet.

Relax. It's too old for them to recognize you.

"I think there's some cash but I didn't look or count it," Hart said. "I just wanted to know who to return it to." He gripped it by one corner and hefted it, as if feeling its weight. "It sure is heavy though. Must be all the leather."

Emily cleared her throat and extended a hand toward the wallet. "It's handmade," she said and pulled her fingers into a fist without touching it. "Probably has cardboard in the middle too." She stopped. Had she said too much?

The other four just looked at her.

"What, haven't you seen a handmade wallet before?" she said. "I remember my dad making them." He'd made that one, and a red one, in those last days while they waited for the new identifications to arrive.

"Does he still make them?" Hart asked. "It's kinda cool."

She did a no-blinking, long-distance stare. "I lost him a long time ago." She rubbed her palms on her thighs.

"Sorry," Hart said. "My dad died too," he said, making the assumption that most people did. "A couple of years ago," he added. He cleared his throat.

"I'm so sorry," Emily said. "It's not easy, is it?" She tucked her hands between her knees and hunched her shoulders in a protective curl.

Hart glanced away, looked back and nodded before pulling out his cell phone. "Who should I call?"

"Call that Conrad fellow," Emily said and fished a business card out of her pocket. "He's the guy who questioned us all, and he's over at the campground right now." She set down the card and with one finger slid it across the table.

Hart picked it up, put it down and peering at it, punched in the numbers.

Seeing the wallet distressed her more than anything that had happened. *Last connection*. Emily waited, concentrating on the hum of voices in the room. If she didn't refocus, she might cry.

Conrad must have answered because Hart told him about the wallet and hung up. "He's going to come and get it," he said. "And he wants to talk to everyone again. All that were at the party." He stood. "I gotta go make some calls so they'll meet him here."

"Well, that's a development," Gwen said and watched Hart start his calls as he headed out to the waterfront patio.

"I did tell the policeman about the party and the kids running from the rain," Emily said. "He said it helped establish the timeline."

Gwen stood. "I think we need dessert and a hot drink. Who wants tea? Coffee?" The order taken she headed for the kitchen.

Emily sat unblinking for long moments, the smell of worked leather and the tap-tap of her father's tools as he worked filling her memory.

"Why was Harvey Conrad at the campground this morning, do you know?" Kelsey asked. "Are there new developments?"

Emily blinked. "Searching my trailer. I had an infestation of frogs overnight." She pulled her nerves into a tight bundle, put on a smile and in a light manner told them about the frogs.

"Wow, that sounds nasty."

"Not the most pleasant morning gift." Emily manufactured a laugh. "It was quite a shock to step out of bed this morning into a herd of croaking intruders."

It was more of a shock that she'd sleep soundly enough for someone to get past her locks, dump in the frogs and seal things up again. Had someone, somehow got in when she wasn't there and put drugs in her hot chocolate? A shiver cascaded over her body.

What do they want? To scare me? Or kill me?

. . . . .

Harvey locked Emily Martin's trailer and pocketed the keys. He walked into the central roadway and looked to the north. How long did it take to release frogs into the wild? Turner and the boys should be back by now. As if on cue, the three came into view at the top of the campground.

Adam carried the frog-box, its hanging position revealing its emptiness. The boys ran ahead of Turner and reached Harvey first.

"Guess what we found?" Adam asked.

"Guess, mess, recess…" Kane rhymed.

Turner reached them, and grinning at Harvey, held up an evidence bag with keys in it.

"We found Mr. Dan's keys," Adam announced.

"I found them," Kane insisted.

Adam rolled his eyes. "Whatever, we have the keys."

Turner held out the bag to Harvey who nodded and returned the grin. Good old Turner and his habit of carrying evidence bags in his pocket. "Good find, fellas."

He pulled coins out of his pocket. "This deserves a reward." He handed the boys each a toonie. "Have a treat on me."

"Yippee, thanks." The boys ran for the canteen.

"We're off to the café," Harvey said. He led the way to the car. "Not only do I need to return Ms. Martin's keys, but Hart Harris has Grady's wallet. I'd like to hear his story."

Turner only nodded and got into the driver's seat.

Harvey powered down his window. He preferred the breeze over the chill wash of air conditioning.

"I found a spying device in the trailer," he said to Turner. "There was a lead and small camera over the kitchen window."

Turner only nodded. The man was as silent as a Sphinx.

"Someone has been watching her. I removed the optic end and I'll give the whole works to the Ident team. Maybe they can figure out where the pictures were going."

The silent Turner looked over at Harvey but said not a word.

CHAPTER 11

At the café they stepped out of the car into direct sun. With no trees to shelter it, the parking lot was an overheated griddle. Not so much as a whisper of a breeze stirred.

Inside the familiar café, Harvey stood watching the room and gradually all heads turned in his direction. Conversation trickled to a stop, the tourists being the last to realize something was happening. Having pinpointed the people he needed to see, Harvey started across the half-full café. He kept his steps measured and nodded at the owner, Wayne, standing at the doors to the kitchen.

His gaze fell on the guide of the local whale tours at Creaser's Cove. He paused at his table. "Jerry, how's business?"

"Good, Harvey, real good."

He moved on to the pulled-together tables occupied by the teens. Pink-streaked hair and multi-studded ears did not carry enough cheekiness to squelch the curiosity about the murder. Half-empty glasses adorned their table, and the kids all leaned in, feet tucked under chairs. One-by-one they looked down as the officers approached.

He'd talked to a couple of them already but would question them again. "Were you all at the party?" Harvey asked, placing his hat on the table.

Some nodded, but others shook their heads.

"I need to talk to all of you from the party. I'll settle in over there." He pointed to a table, "I want to talk to you one at a time. You first Hart."

Harvey headed for the empty table. Just beyond it, four women occupied the last table—Gwen Harris, wife of the owner, Devon Ritcey, wife of Greg Cunningham over at the Caleb Cove Security Agency and Kelsey Maxwell, wife of Greg's partner, Sam Logan. And the last one—Emily Martin. *How has she ended up with that group*?

Emily stared at him, he could see her gaze focused in his direction, and a frown creasing her brow. The others glanced over but did not stare. He greeted them as a group. "Ladies."

Harvey reached his goal, removed his hat and flipped a chair around so that he straddled it like he had the picnic bench the day before. Turner pulled back a chair and sat off to the side, taking out his notebook and pen.

Harvey motioned for Hart to join him. "Now Hart," he said as Hart sat across from him, "let's see that wallet."

Hart placed the wallet on the table. "I looked inside," he volunteered.

Harvey grunted. "I'll need to get your fingerprints," he said. "Don't know what they'll be able to get off this, but we'll need them for elimination." He pulled out a pair of gloves and opened the wallet. It took him about forty-five seconds to check the contents. He snapped it shut and set it down. "Damn," he muttered.

"Is there anything useful?" Hart asked.

"Not much," Harvey muttered. *I've never met anyone with less contact to the digital world than this guy*. He shook his head, checked over his shoulder to be sure Turner was ready with notebook and pen. "Tell me about that night."

Hart drummed his fingers on the table then grabbed one hand with the other, clutching them into stillness. "Not much to tell. We were running to get out of the rain. I kicked something on the path and picked it up." He pointed at the wallet. "That's it."

"Running from where?" Harvey asked, even though he already knew.

"A fire pit up the beach. Just before the point."

"Time?" Confirmation from several sources was always better than one.

"Must have been after midnight. I dropped a couple of people off then went home and I was there by one a.m."

"You're sure?"

Hart nodded. "It's when I agreed to be home, so I looked when I got in."

Harvey continued. "What about earlier? When you were headed out to the party. You went down through that path?"

Hart nodded.

"Who was around then?"

Hart scratched his head.

"Just think back," Harvey said. "Start where you parked and walk your memory forward."

Hart splayed his fingers on the table and stared at them. "We parked up at the lot beside the office. Lenya was there, she stuck her head out to say hi. I was carrying the cooler." He lifted a guilty gaze to Harvey.

"I'm not going to ask what was in the cooler," Harvey said.

Hart toggled his head. "Two of the guys went ahead of me." He frowned. "There was a guy," he said. "He was just by the trees at the edge of the path. He was bird-dogging the place."

"Bird-dogging?"

"Still as a post. Head up and titled like he was listening. What caught my attention was that he sniffed – a couple of times – like a dog does."

"Would you recognize the guy?"

Hart clicked his tongue. "It was shaded and already quite dark. Didn't really see his face. But I think it was Mr. Grady."

"So, you knew Dan Grady?"

"Not really. But he's been to the cove a couple of times a summer for the past few years. Wayne let him set up in the parking lot. He came over for ice cream sometimes." Hart paused. "And one time, he helped me fix my bike. You know, before I got my truck."

Was there anything about him that might help with identifying him?"

"He was wearing a cap."

"Baseball type?"

"Yes."

"And there was no cell phone with the wallet?"

"Not that I saw."

Harvey nodded. They needed to search around where the wallet had been found. "If you think of anything else, give me call." He handed over one of his cards. "Now I need to talk to the others. Two guys you said."

"And the girls." Hart contributed, pointing across the room. "They came in Tammy's car after us. I think they came out to the beach by the other end of the campground. You know, where the other path goes through the end of the woods straight onto the rocks."

Harvey glanced at the group in the front corner. "Send Tammy over for starters." Might as well begin with a chatty person.

. . . . .

Emily chewed her lip as Conrad interviewed the teens. Each of them moved quickly to the hot-seat willing to tell what they could. She picked at her blueberry grunt, not tasting the blueberry sauce or the steamed dumplings. If she chewed, she had less chance of overhearing.

If only I'd come back sooner from my walk. She might have run into Dan, and he wouldn't have been out in the woods in the night. He'd have been in her trailer with her.

Don't beat yourself up. He might have been there anyway. You don't know for sure he was coming to see you.

She tucked her feet under her chair with ankles crossed, and leaned on the table, hunching her shoulders forward. Who was she kidding? He'd been coming to see her. That's why they were both in this fishbowl of a place—to meet, to talk, to catch up. *And, if I'd had my way, to reveal who the hell I really am.*

She shifted her gaze, taking in the action around the room. The teens at the corner table were talking among themselves, quieter now that the initial excitement was over. What had they seen?

Conrad seemed to be tracking his way through the interviews. Had the kids talked it over? Would their evidence be contaminated by the comparing notes? *Not my problem. And yet it is. It's my damn father that's dead.* She cleared her throat and looked down, hiding tears that sprang unbidden to her eyes.

Conrad conferred with his fellow officer, nodded and standing, pulled his hat onto his head, anchoring it with a tug. "Thanks," he commented to the room in general.

The two officers stopped beside Gwen. "Good day, ladies." Harvey nodded to include Emily. "Here's your keys. Could I speak with you for a minute?"

Reluctantly curious, Emily nodded and stood. Conrad pointed to the patio doors and preceding her there, opened the door for her.

"What's wrong?" Emily asked.

"I did find a camera lead in your trailer," Harvey said.

Emily felt her face freeze. Someone was watching her? "What?"

"I removed it," Harvey said. "I've asked for the technicians to see if they can figure out where the transmissions are going. They won't need to get inside and it should be taken care of by supper time."

Emily gulped. "I can go back though? Right?"

"It'd be better if you went somewhere else for a couple of nights."

She shook her head. "I'll be okay."

"Oh, and you don't have any hot chocolate," Conrad said. "I took it to have it tested, just in case."

So she wasn't the only one worried about her being drugged. "Thanks."

"Put me on speed dial," he said. "Call for anything, we'll get the unit out there. There'll be one in this area tonight."

Emily frowned. The police were turning out to be pretty obliging. She chewed the inside of her lip. Fine. She'd trust him with watching her, but not with anything more.

She wanted to ask about the camper, about the investigation. But as far as the officers knew, she'd only found the body. And she wasn't about to reveal her connection now, not after having hidden it and after telling quite a few lies, well almost lies, to Constable Harvey Conrad.

Conrad held the door open again. Another myth busted. Cops could be gentlemen.

"Be careful," Conrad said. "See you around." He nodded to Turner and they headed for the front.

Emily almost laughed. "Sure," she said, *but not if I see you first.* She returned to her seat.

. . . . .

The front door jangled behind the officers, and Hart pushed away from the corner table where he'd retreated after his interview. Emily looked up as he joined her and the other women at their table. Did he need a session of the *Touched by Murder Club*?

"Thought you might want to know what we saw." Hart sat and leaned back, one arm hooked over the back of the chair. He jiggled one leg, drummed fingers on the chair arm. "I saw a man in the woods when we were headed over to the party. And Tammy," he said, indicating the other table with a twitch of his head. "She saw another guy."

Without asking if they wanted to know, he raised a hand. "Hey, Tammy, come here a sec, would you?"

His jiggling escalated. Looked like he had a serious adrenaline rush going on. She knew that feeling.

Tammy, the clerk from the grocery store, joined them, pink hair, earrings and all. "Hey," she said to Emily. "You'll need more chocolate after this, eh?" She pulled over a chair and grabbed the back of it with both hands and literally danced behind it. "Man, this is wild," she said.

Hart waved at her. "Sit, tell them about the guy you saw."

She sat. "Well, the officer said it might not be related. But there was this guy at the edge of the woods behind the campsites, but over by the beach side, you know? I just caught a glimpse. I remembered him because he stood so still. He was looking through the woods but he glanced over when we came out of the path."

Tammy shivered. "His eyes were creepy. It was as if he looked right through me. But then he pulled his cap down. One of those fishing hat types with a brim all around." She sighed dramatically and sat back, obviously enjoying the attention. "Oh," she said, "and he had a tat. It showed below his sleeve." She indicated a spot on her arm just above her wrist. "And continued up on his neck." She shook one hand. "Man, it was some serious ink."

Emily's brain twigged. A tat? On his wrist? The waiter at the wedding reception had had a tat like that.

Kelsey sat forward. "What was the picture?"

"I wasn't close enough to tell, but it had color in it."

"Too bad," Kelsey said. "It might have helped find him."

Hart glanced at the wall clock. "I gotta go. I'm on duty in twenty minutes." He stood and shoved in his chair. "Stop by later for some ice cream." And with a wave of his hand he headed to the boardwalk behind the café and his ice cream stand.

Tammy nodded. "Nice to see you again, Emily. See you around." And she rejoined her friends at the front table.

Emily finished her coffee. If it was the same tattoo, the same man, he might be the stalker.

"You okay?" Devon asked.

Emily smiled and put her napkin on the table. "Sure. But as nice as this had been, I'd better get going." She pushed back her chair.

The others stood as well and, as she started to leave, each one stopped her for a hug. Embarrassment washed over her as she stiffly accepted the hugs. That was more people-touching than she'd had in over a year.

Gwen handed her a card. "This has all our cell phone numbers. You call if you need anything, even just some company."

Overwhelmed, Emily took the card. "Thanks." She put it in her pocket. It was an amazing gesture as far as she was concerned. Not that'd she call them.

As if reading her mind, Kelsey touched her lightly on the shoulder. "And if you don't call us, we'll come looking for you." She laughed, but Emily could tell she was serious. Who were these women? How could they accept her so readily without knowing anything about her, other than she'd found a dead man?

"And remember," Devon said, "be here about 10:30 tomorrow for coffee. Lem will be taking the bus tour people on a walking tour of town. I'll let him know you'll be tagging along. It'll take your mind off things."

"Ah, thanks," Emily said again. She gave a small wave. "See you around." Now she was sounding like the Caleb Cove residents. Or Caleb's Cove as they all preferred.

She shifted her mini-knapsack style purse onto her shoulder and walked away. Remembering another knapsack, one filled with fifty thousand dollars, and another walking away took her back in time. What had her dad done with the rest of the money? He couldn't be lugging it around and anything she'd seen didn't indicate he was spending much of it.

She paused before pushing open the exit door. *Hey, with your dad dead, you can lead a normal life. No need to protect him anymore. That's what you wanted, isn't it? Not the money?*

But instead of relief, sorrow washed over her, and her shoulders sagged. The money might not matter, but the information about her personal history did. Her dad and mother must have had families. She pushed out into the parking lot and the wide vacant afternoon. Somewhere she might have grandparents or uncles or cousins. Gone, gone, all gone. Her throat ached. Family. What would it like to have people with shared history, shared genetics, similar features or habits?

The taste of camaraderie she'd just shared with the murder club had given her a taste of what she'd never have. She might have been better not knowing, not coming here at all.

. . . . .

Outside the café, Harvey stepped into August heat that continued to bear down on real estate, humans and the odd stray cat. The simple walk to the car produced moisture on his forehead. He wiped it with the back of his hand and looked toward the water. "How about an ice cream cone, Turner?"

Turner nodded and followed Harvey around the building to the boardwalk between café and marina. Hart's ice cream stand faced the ocean and Harvey stepped up to the counter.

A red-head teenager stood beside Hart. "What'll it be, officers?" he asked.

Harvey looked at all the varieties. "One scoop of chocolate and one of vanilla, please." He turned to Turner. "You want the usual."

Turner nodded and Harvey ordered. "One of those orange and licorice things for him."

Moments later, cones in hand, Harvey and Turner paced out along the boat slips. A small sailing boat had just docked and Jeff Brown was tying her fast.

Harvey grinned. Constable Parker might not be finding any drug runners, but she sure was getting a tan. He watched as she and Jeff Brown prepared the boat for the night. Not a word was spoken. Obviously the sailing lessons were taking effect and Parker knew what to do. Seemed that Brown, a computer wizard in his day job, had other talents.

Harvey waited until they were finished. "Any luck today?" he asked.

Parker turned to meet him. "Not much. But there is a cove with two derelict fishing boats and an old building and it's a position of interest, I'd say."

Turner edged around them and started asking boat type questions of Jeff Brown. Harvey and Parker strolled back toward the café patio.

"It's the haunted house that Lem talks about," Parker said. "It's just inland from those abandoned boats. We're waiting to find out owns the land. At the moment, all we know is they are from Montreal and paid cash for the land."

"Fair enough. A haunted house legend would be enough to either keep people away, or these days, lure them in to check it out."

"True enough. But the locals are no longer interested and the others who hear the story are usually the bus tourists who get the history and ghost tour from Lem. After the tour, they all get on the bus and leave."

"How modern. Ghosts that help the local economy."

Parker nodded. "Word on the street in Halifax is that there's a large shipment coming in about a month. Not sure if it's coming in through here or not. We hope to nail that down before-times and then we'll get a take-down operation in place. We've narrowed the possible transporters down to two. The grocery delivery van and the carpenters working on that house over on the next island. Our undercover man made good contact up in the city. We might be able to find out who is the on-site organizer here."

Harvey raised his eyebrows. "So, one step forward, two back is it?"

Parker nodded. "We had considered the bike man, especially after he was murdered, because that trailer of his would hold quite a bit. But I talked to the investigators. Nothing in there but bikes, parts and tools. And no residue of any kind."

Harvey stopped where the pier joined the boardwalk. "I interviewed a Lydia Mason at the campground. She might be a link to the suppliers. She shows signs of use and her sons mentioned that she meets a man on the beach. Might be worth watching."

He looked over his shoulder at the boats. "Are you getting the intel you need?"

She laughed. "And then some. Jeff is amazing on the computers over at the Security Agency. Some of the things he gets, I avoid asking the source."

"Handy fellow," Harvey said and grinned at her. "Sailing instructor, hi-tech computer geek. Anything I'm missing?"

Parker frowned. "That is all." But she did blush.

Harvey popped the last bit of cone into his mouth and turned back to the boat slips. He swallowed, licked his lips and whistled to get Turner's attention. The other officer headed back. Harvey nodded to Parker. "We'll all keep an eye out," he said. "You'll get a lead in time. I'll be able to give you more help, once we tie up this murder."

"So you're sure it was murder?"

Harvey lifted one shoulder and let it drop. "Maybe. Hard to tell. He was almost dead of cancer and quite weak. He might have fallen. But the evidence tells us the place was searched after he was on the floor." He fished a toothpick from his shirt pocket and stuck it in his mouth.

Parker rocked on her feet. "Ah. Hum. So you know who he is?"

"No, no luck there either. We have some uniforms doing door to door at the oncologists' offices and cancer clinics as well as checking pharmacies. One of the meds is unusual, but no one has identified his photo yet."

Parker turned back toward the water. "Good luck with it. You'll get a lead sooner or later. And hey, thanks for the tip about Lydia Mason. If you get a description of the man the kids saw, let me know. We have three men on our suspect list and a description could narrow things down."

She headed toward Turner and Jeff Brown on the boat slip.

Harvey waited until Turner joined him and led the way back to the front of the buildings. Just another day in the life of a police officer. He sighed. One day soon he'd like a civilian life. A quick memory of Emily Martin wrapped around him flashed through him. One of the perks of being a police officer. He grinned. On second thought, no way was he giving up policing.

CHAPTER 12

Emily cradled a mug of coffee and pressed her shoulders against the wall at the back of the café. Her sleep had been rocky and she'd wakened with stiff muscles, gritty eyes and a threatening headache. Her earlier shower and now the coffee were barely dragging her into a decent frame of mind.

Most of the café tables were occupied with white-haired, well-padded seniors. Dave Lamont's floral shirt drew her attention. Was he joining the tour today? And in the far front corner, a man who looked familiar sat alone at a table. Where had she seen him? Oh, right. She'd seen him talking to the lady who owned the grocery store. It had not looked like a friendly conversation. Was he there for the tour, or just a coffee?

Lem Ritcey entered through the back patio doors, apparently ready for the history lesson and ghost tour. Emily sipped coffee as he greeted Gwen who brought him over for an introduction. Lem helped the local economy by attracting bus tours full of tourists with his stories of rum running, ghost ships and cultural minutiae.

"Welcome to the tour," Lem said and shook her hand. "Do you like history?"

Emily nodded. "Yes, in particular I enjoy family histories." Might as well establish a baseline for asking questions.

"Good," Lem said, "history here is entwined with families." He grinned. "We also have a few ghosts."

"My favorite type of families," she said.

Lem made his way to the side of the room. One after another, the tour participants stopped talking, and Lem began his spiel.

Emily listened, alert for what she didn't really know. Maybe it was one of those situations where she'd know what she was looking for when she heard it. The early settlement of the area, from the late 1600s up through the 1800s, and the fishing and farming in the area, counted for expansion. The 1800s and the pirate stories introduced the warships of the War of 1812 and ghost ships, forerunners and curses.

"Oak Island is the most famous location and hundreds have searched the island for treasure. Our islands here saw their own action and goods from shipwrecks washed up on shore. On the third island, so many ships washed onto the reefs that lumber littered the shores." Lem's deep compelling voice held his audience, Emily included, enthralled.

"One enterprising chap gathered the lumber over a few years and built a house with it." Lem paused, shook his head and cast his gaze downward. "Unfortunately, when he moved in, he found the ghosts of drowned sailors occupying the place. Finally, on the verge of being driven crazy, he moved out."

"Is the house still there?" asked a woman at the front table.

"Yes, most of it."

"Can we go and see it?"

Lem shook his head. "The bus can't make it across the last bridge. When we get to the museum at the end of the tour, you can read the full story and see the wall posters of the place. There are several galleries with photos and stories of the history around here."

Emily revised her assumption that the museum was a simple collection of local items. Sounded like someone had put some work into the place.

Lem came to the more current history of the 1900s and the prohibition years. "Rum runners made good money," he said. "My uncle was only fourteen years old, but he and his buddies ran surf boats to bring the booze ashore from the ships. Good money in the enterprise. He never revealed how much he made, but he lived better than his younger brothers. He obviously had a nest egg that got him started in life." Laughter rippled around the room.

"The kegs of rum, or the cases of bottles, were sometimes stored in caves until transport was arranged up province. Those caves were, and are, dangerous places. The only one I ever visited had its mouth below water at high tide. The interior was higher then and they'd put in an airshaft that ran up through the cliff to the surface. Quite an elaborate place." He stopped for a drink of water. "And before you ask," he said with a smile, "we can't go there either. Too dangerous and too small and too darn difficult to get to."

The woman in the front raised her hand. "I thought the tour guide said we would go to some caves."

Lem nodded. "That would be The Ovens, a large group of caves further down the shore."

He went on with his stories. "Other times they simply buried the cargo in the sand dunes. That was riskier, not only because of possible detection, but also because those picking up the haul occasionally missed a barrel. For a few decades after, people would stumble across some of the illegal booty."

He held up one of the brochures and opened it to the middle. "If you have your map, you can follow along as we walk down the road. We'll go out through the patio to the boardwalk for information on the harbor and then it's down the road to one of the original houses. If anyone has difficulty walking for about ten minutes, speak up. We have two golf carts and a couple of young fellows to drive you." He paused but no one asked for help.

"After the house, which by the way is my family home, five generations of Ritceys have lived there, we'll go see the manse and old church. The church was decommissioned about a decade ago and now is a gift store.

"Nancy, the owner, has preserved what she could, and pictures of how it used to be, along with some wedding photos of older residents, line the walls. The one thing they did replace was the bell in the tower. It now has a siren used to call everyone together for emergencies."

"What kind of emergencies do you have?" asked the little women in the front.

"Fire, missing children, someone missing on the water…things like that." Lem grinned. "We don't use it very often, thank goodness." He looked around at his charges. "We'll take a break there for you to browse and then we'll move on to the graveyard." He paused, flipped the folder shut and raised one eyebrow. "At the graveyard we'll visit the grave responsible for the cove's name and its deadly curse."

Curse? Was that the one that Gwen had mentioned yesterday? Emily deposited her cup in the dirty-dishes tray and prepared to follow the crowd. This was turning out to be more interesting than she'd expected and a welcome relief from the incessant questioning in her brain.

. . . . .

When they got to the Ritcey homestead, Emily spent her time standing on the veranda and looking out to sea. She rejoined the group as the height of the afternoon sun lowered to half-mast. The church-turned-store had a wide range of local and other Canadian items. Emily bought nothing. She needed nothing and had no one to buy for.

The graveyard might no longer be in use, but gravel paths wound among the memorial stones and neatly clipped grass covered the graves. Lem led them to a section where stones with almost erased engravings announced local names, and dates back to the 1700s.

"Take your time and read the stones," Lem said. "Take note of the names and you can track them on the family-tree charts in the museum when we get there. Our goal is help history come alive. Not only have we been able to trace families back hundreds of years, but we've also been able to collect family heirlooms and photos from many of those families."

Emily wandered away from the group. Family trees, history and pictures were invaluable when tracing a family tree. Usually, she was given the last branch on the tree and traced it back in time for her clients. Working on the premise that Dan had brought her here for a specific reason, perhaps for her own family history, she'd have to hope that somehow, something in the past would speak to her and lead her to the present.

She shuddered. And given that someone here apparently knew her gave validity to her premise. Whoever was watching her had referred to the sins of the father. Wasn't the additional part of that about the children paying? She needed to find more information before her unknown watcher upped his game. He'd progressed from notes and candy to snakes and frogs. What would be his next move, and more critical, what final game did he have planned?

"Okay folks, come on over. Two specific graves to talk about and then we'll head over to the museum."

Lem stood beside a tall stone, its arching top supporting a figurehead similar to those mounted on the prow of old-fashioned ships. As they gathered around him, he pointed to the name. "Caleb Krause," he said, "died during a robbery at his home back in 1865. Two men had broken in and the ten-year-old, presumably wakened by their noise, got up and wandered out to the upper hall. In the ensuing mix-up, he fell over the banister rail and hit the floor in the entry below. His neck was snapped."

A gasp and sigh of sympathy went through the crowd.

Lem continued. "His heartbroken mother buried him here. When his sea-captain father returned from his voyage, he took the figurehead from his ship and mounted it here to guard his oldest son. The mother never recovered. She later put a curse on the two men and within six months the two were murdered in Lunenburg. On her death bed, the mother extended the curse to cover any evil-intentioned person who put foot on this island, Dane's Island. It was intended to keep her younger son, Dane, safe."

"The cove became known as Caleb's Cove, although the map makers later listed it as Caleb Cove. And the curse remains." He laid a finger on one side of his nose, and winked. "More than one crook has died here. Interestingly enough, only one man died during the rum running years. He'd tried to double-cross his partners. Apparently the ghosts approved of spirits." A laugh rumbled through the crowd.

He left his spot and walked across the back of the graveyard, the tourists trailing after him. "Caleb's grave was the first and the graveyard grew up around it." Near the fence, Lem stopped and knelt beside a small stone embedded in the grass. The name was clear and easy to see. *Not an old stone.*

"This," he said, "is the last grave. It is for a young woman brought home from a terrible accident in Montreal."

Emily edged around the crowd, an urge she couldn't define, drawing her closer to the stone. She paused just beyond Lem's crouched figure. White flowers surrounded the plot. *Lilies.* The date was the year Suzie-before-she-was-Emily had turned five. One name adorned the stone. *Lily.*

She slapped a hand over her moth to halt the gasp threatening to erupt. Her stomach caved and chills raced over her skin.

My mother.

The words erupted in her head, blocking sight, sound and smell and Emily crumpled.

. . . . .

By the time Emily recovered from her weak turn, many of the tourists had left for the museum. Emily, and the little woman with the questions, arrived at the tail end of the group. Emily pulled open one of the double doors and entered the museum lobby shoulder to shoulder with the woman. *Like two gunslingers entering a saloon.* Old-wood scent and freshly scrubbed mustiness tickled her nose. The door closed behind her, and hints of times past crowded her. The place reeked of history, but it pulled her back to her conscious present.

How did I get here? Obviously she'd walked, but she remember only snatches since she'd sunk to the ground at the graveyard. The nearly passing out had not gone unnoticed. Several of the seniors, along with Dave Lamont, had rushed to her when she'd collapsed to a crouch. The woman currently by her side had taken charge and made the others back off to give Emily air. She'd knelt beside Emily, pulled a small bottle out of her bag and administered smelling salts. The potent smell had had Emily coughing and tearing up. Dave had helped her up.

"Are you okay now, dear?" asked the woman, patting Emily's arm.

Emily nodded. "Thank you so much for your help. I don't know what came over me."

The woman leaned in and whispered. "Maybe woman things and too much heat."

Emily let it go at that. She barely believed what she'd seen and thought. How could she explain that to anyone? "I need to go to the washroom" she said. "I could do with some cold water on my face." The woman made as if to accompany her.

"I'll be fine," Emily said. "You go and join your friends. I'll catch up."

The woman looked Emily in the eye. "Are you sure?"

"Very sure." Emily smiled at her benefactor, a grandmotherly type, and turning, located the washroom signs. She itched to get at those family trees, but she needed stability before she did. Cold water, both on face and in her stomach, would do the trick. As least, she hoped it would.

In the washroom, she took long moments to stare in the mirror. Her mother had died in an accident in Montreal. How did that fit with her father's story of theft and bad guys? And apparently they'd brought her here, to her home, for burial. Shivers ran up and down her arms. How close was she to finding out the rest of her story?

. . . . .

The man let the throng of fussy, old people enter the building before he turned and walked rapidly away. That damn gravestone. How had he not known it was there? That, and those frigging family trees and photos, might give the girl too much information before he made his move. He muttered curses under his breath and ground one fist into the other palm. His plan hinged on her needing help to get her information. His help. He needed her jumpy and edgy. Now that was funny. He was the one jumpy and edgy. Maybe he needed his meds. He kicked a can some inconsiderate litterbug had left on the side of the road. It spun away into the ditch.

I know the truth of it all. She needs to talk to me. She just doesn't know it yet. A plan to advance his agenda formed in his head. He'd have to keep a close eye on her and wait for the right moment. But it had to be soon. Tonight would be best. He needed a big distraction on his side.

He glanced back toward the museum. He'd made a quick tour through it when he'd arrived. Then he had been checking to see if any old pictures of his teenaged sojourn in the cove remained. He crossed the road and found his vehicle. If they were there, they were well buried, and he'd ceased worrying about them. Besides, he didn't look like that pathetic, skinny, bespectacled kid anymore.

Most of the family trees were filed on poster board in one of those big display units where they put pictures to be flipped through. There had to be close to a hundred of them. All he could do was hope she didn't hit the right one before the museum closed. Or that Lily and Dan were never entered on the correct family tree. He glanced at his watch. Only thirty minutes left. He looked skyward. *For Pete's sake, don't let her find them.*

. . . . .

Stabilized by water splashed on her face and a long drink at the fountain, Emily rejoined the group in the vaulted lobby.

Lem was making an announcement. "Usually, we close at five," he said, "but we'll stay open for about an hour so you can browse the displays here on the main floor. I'll be around if you have questions." He motioned to a woman behind him, and she stepped forward. "This is Lenya, one of Caleb's descendants and, like me, one of the sixty-somethings left here. We'll both be available to answer questions."

"What's up the stairs?" The questioning woman was back on the job.

Lem looked toward the sweeping oak staircase with a rope across the bottom. "Records," he said, "and photos—items that still require sorting and labeling."

"So we can't go up?"

He shook his head and smiled. "Not much point unless you're a researcher and don't mind getting really dusty."

Emily could get dirty and she'd searched in many a stash of photos and documents. She joined the group as they wandered through the main level. *And do I have questions? Damn straight I do.* But was she ready to ask them? Excitement and fear thrummed along her nerves and upped-up her heartrate. *How much information can I assimilate in one afternoon?* Good question.

Lem and Lenya stepped off to the side and Emily felt Lem's gaze on her. When she met it, he turned to Lenya. Obviously they were talking about Emily. He was probably telling Lenya about her weak turn and she'd put money on Lenya checking on her later in the evening. A squiggly warmth snaked down her spine. A pleasant warmth that left her feeling safe. People here noticed things and helped each other. She could get used to that.

Emily followed the group and stared at the pictures and plaques, without grasping the content. She peered into display cases holding early sextants and ropes and household items. And she walked away from the cases unable to remember a thing she'd looked at.

It's all interesting, but where are the family trees? She turned and headed back to the main hall. There, where she had obviously missed them in the beginning, two huge family charts stretched from floor level up through the vaulted area. She approached the first one.

Why am I holding my breath?
Because I'm afraid?
But afraid of what? Finding family or not finding them?

For a long moment she stared down at the floor and, summoning her nerve, looked up. The print at the top was larger and she could read it easily. The chart she'd chosen was Caleb's family. Quickly she scanned down through the generations that spilled along the limbs from Caleb's younger brother, Dane. On the bottom she found Lenya with two daughters, Gwen and Gayle. Gwen's marriage to Wayne Harris was recorded and their two children, Jude and Jemma. Her sister, Gayle, showed no marriage.

Emily went back a level on the chart. Lenya had one brother. Another level up showed that Lenya's mother had had three siblings. Lenya's two uncles showed family down through several grandchildren. Gwen and her sister had a lot of cousins. *Lucky sods.*

Lenya's aunt, Esther, had married a Harry Gerber. He died only ten years after their wedding. There were lines leading down, but no children listed. Were there no children? Or had they never been entered?

She traced back up more slowly, looking at the family names carried forward and early deaths of the men. Had they died at sea? She sighed and turned away. Her body slumped slightly and the urge to close her eyes and sleep grew strong in her head. *Frogs yesterday, a walking tour, graves, a shock...too much all at once.*

Lem rang a bell on the counter and people gathered from various corners. "Well folks, that's the story of Caleb's Cove and some of the history of the area. Thanks for visiting and come back any time." He ushered them all, Emily included, out the door.

CHAPTER 13

Good news—I found a clue to my family. Bad news—my mother is dead. The faint hope that had lingered in a corner of Emily's being, had died when she saw that gravestone. The image of the flat stone blipped across her memory. She blinked. She'd reached the turn into the campground. No memory of the main road, or the corner onto the secondary road, came to her. Not good. She'd been driving lost in a haze.

She parked the truck, locked it and headed for the trailer. At the door, she hesitated. The place had been violated and bugged. Constable Conrad had searched it. *Contaminated twice.* She shuddered. *No longer a safe haven.* The path to the ocean ran behind her, and a glimpse of blue with white-capped waves beckoned her. She returned to the truck, put her purse under the driver's seat and locked the door. Her head buzzed, but her body needed movement and fresh air. She strode down the path, looked left and right, and headed left toward the point. Out at the end she'd find a breeze brisk enough to swipe away any fog.

The jumble of rocks had a path of stepping stones leading out to the ocean. Irregular enough to be crafted by nature, they were smooth enough to handle her footsteps. When water lapped at the rocks, stirring seaweed in undulating waves, she stopped. *End of the rocks.* She turned back and checked the area. Off to her right, a shelf formed by two boulders offered her an ideal seating place. Cleansing breezes buffeted her. Warm sunlight engulfed her. The waves slurped and slushed providing ocean music that washed away her brain fog and her body tension.

For long moments she let her mind sink into nothingness. But like those pesky squirrels in a carnival game, the thoughts popped up. *My mother's grave. Records of families. Generations of legends.* Hope returned. She'd return to the museum when it opened in the morning and start reading all the family trees. There had to be clues there.

Her dad had died before telling her what she wanted to know. She'd left it too late. On the other hand, she had no reason to protect him anymore. And if others were seeking the cash-stash left from their crime, they were out of luck. A vision of piles of money-bundles stacked in the living room of her teens flashed in her head. Her father had given her fake ID turning her eighteen overnight and giving her a drivers' license and high school diploma. In truth, she'd been about to turn sixteen. He'd added a backpack filled with cash—fifty thousand dollars' worth—and sent her off on her own. What had he done with the rest of the money?

The thought poked at her, demanding that she face it. More to the point, where had all that money come from? She knew he'd stolen it, and that explained the running and the avoidance of law enforcement. But why was he more afraid of others? Who had he stolen from?

Her belief system was solidly grounded in the police as an enemy. But now, with the logic of an adult, she knew that belief was false. Still, it was difficult, uncomfortable even, to think about turning to the police for help. She really needed to get over that. A smile tugged at her lips. Maybe hanging out with Harvey Conrad would make trusting police easier.

The sun glinted on the rolling waves and drew her attention. The scene out to the horizon looked like it was out of a movie. Beautiful. If she was from here, she could accept that easily.

She sighed. Was her stalker one of the other thieves? She massaged her temples with her fingertips. If so, they were out of luck. She didn't have the information, or the money.

But what was he, or she, trying to prove with notes and frogs and spying on her. Okay, she got the spying. They were checking to see if she produced the money behind closed doors. For some reason they were in her face so to speak. They knew what she was doing. Scary thought.

A thump behind her triggered her to turn and look. Hart was making his way toward her. He raised a hand.

"Hey, great day to stare at the waves, eh?" He took one last hop and stood on the top of her rock. "Okay if I join you?"

She shuffled to one side and he slid down to sit beside her.

"How did you enjoy the tour?" he asked.

She frowned at him. How did he know that?

As if he'd read her mind, he laughed. "In Caleb's Cove, everyone knows every other person's business sooner or later. Gwen told me when I was at the café today."

"No ice cream stand this evening?"

"Redd is taking his shift. I've been training him and another teen to take over."

"And then what will you do?"

"EMS," he said. "I've been studying and taking classes. It'll be awhile yet, but it's what I want to do for now. In the long run, I'll be a doctor. I start pre-med in the fall, so Redd and his buddy will take over the ice cream stand until we close it down on Thanksgiving weekend."

Emily looked over the water. "May I ask you about your father?" she asked.

Hart sighed. "Sure. It's been a few years now."

"Did he die here, on this island?"

"Yup, came home dead, he did."

"What?"

"Old saying," Hart explained. "He washed up on shore, dead, like sailors in the olden days when they went into the ocean and drowned. If their body was found, they…"

"…came home dead." She chimed in on the last words. "There are a lot of sayings around here."

"You have no idea. There is a book full of them, an actual published book."

"Okay then. Coming back to your father. Did he drown?"

Hart nodded. "But not without help. He was murdered."

So Hart had lived through what she had as far as losing his father. What were the odds of finding someone else in that category? Of course, from what she'd learned, murder wasn't a stranger here on the island.

"Ah, yes, therefore you are a member of the Touched by Murder Club."

"Card carrying," he said, and drawing up one knee, he stared out to sea.

Silence took over for long minutes.

"What do you think of the legend?" Emily asked. "About the

curse and bad guys."

Hart barked out a laugh. "Who knows? It was true in my dad's case," he said. "Oh yes, white collar crime, but he could be called a criminal for sure."

"It must have been difficult. How did you handle it?" She'd take any suggestions to help her come to grips with her father, his past and his death.

Hart tugged on his earlobe. "My mom helped me. She showed me that I am not my father and I am not responsible for what he did. I loved him. He was my dad and we had some great times. But did I like what he did? No way. Two separate things. Why? Did your dad do something criminal?"

Emily paused. Could she tell him the whole story? She wouldn't even know where to start.

Hey Hart. Dan Grady was my father and a thief.
Hey Hart, funny story about my life...
Hey Hart, my name is a lie....

Faced with actually saying any of it out loud, she panicked. Maybe it wasn't a good idea. "Yes, I don't know what he did exactly, but he ended up with a lot money. Millions. Not his money."

Hart whistled. "That's a lot. Makes loving him hard, doesn't it? But try thinking about him the way my mom said. Separate the man you knew as your father from the deeds he did."

Separate the father part from the deeds he did as crook. *Comforting thought.* "I think I can do that. He was really good to me, and I have fun memories aside from the…well you know."

Hart chucked her on the shoulder. "That's the spirit.

A siren rose and fell, drifting over the water. Three blasts, a space and three more. What the heck? That was first she'd heard it since she'd arrived.

Hart jumped up and pulled out his phone. He pressed one button. Who did he have on speed dial?

"Lem, what's up?" He listened. "What, fire? Who the hell would set the museum on fire? I'm on my way."

No, not the museum. The scream sounded only in Emily's head. She scrambled to her feet. "Fire? At the museum?" Her gut contracted and her breath came in short sips.

"Looks like arson, apparently. We have a volunteer fire department. I gotta go."

"Could I help?"

"Come on, Lenya organizes the women."

He leaped two rocks at once and Emily followed.

Oh crap, oh crap. Just when she thought she was getting somewhere, fate slapped her in the face. *Fate or your stalker?* She knew what he wanted. But did he know what she wanted? If he'd set the fire, he knew.

And if he set the fire, would he be there to watch?

. . . . .

Emily noted Hart's head swivel left and then right even as he swerved around the corner onto the main road. Her vision blurred and her hand tightened on the handhold above the truck door. Now that they were facing south, she fixed her sights on the thin corkscrew of gray-black smoke spiraling against the rapidly darkening night sky. A black and gray kaleidoscope marking the destruction of the orange flames.

"No wind for a change," Hart muttered, "that's good."

Fire in the museum. Emily sucked in her stomach, and held her breath, pressing down the fear forming in her being. *The files, the family trees, the photos. How much fire? How much destruction?*

A whimper escaped. The danger, the destruction, the hopes dashed—so much gone. What could they do? *All that information I needed. Gone.* Heat roared in her head. Where was the fire hall? Was there a county station?

"Who fights fires here?" she asked, her voice strained and raised to be heard over the truck engine.

"Everyone." Hart bit out the word. "Volunteers. We have a plan. The units from Bridgewater are often called out as well, but it takes them thirty minutes to get here." He leaned forward and stayed there intent on the road ahead.

I did that when I was little. I thought it would make the car go faster.

Her body leaned into the forward motion of the truck even as her logical mind reminded her it wasn't true. But although it might not help them go faster, it helped her feel they were making progress.

The trees gave way to the cleared area at the edge of the village. The truck lights swept over the double front doors of the museum. A smoke monster twirled out of the building and, with an abrupt change of direction, became part of the ever rising pillar of smoke.

A hose snaked around the side of the building, pulsing and jerking as water filled it. Two men in firefighting gear held its head. Water burst from its mouth and cascaded onto the building, dark arcs in the night air.

"That's Jackson and Sam," Hart yelled as they passed, as if their identity and presence reassured him. Beyond the museum, the jellybean line of shops sat hunched in the dusk, unaffected by the action. At the café, Hart hauled left on the steering wheel, tromped on the brake and skidded into the lot. He parked behind rows of cars and was out of the vehicle and moving before the truck engine pinged it last rotation.

"Find Lenya," he called and joined an ant-like line of people heading toward the fire.

Emily stood by the truck watching the smoke, the shadowed men at the fire and the women hurrying into the café. *Organized chaos. And yet they are all acting with purpose, no hesitation, no stumbling over each other. They've done this before—or practiced.*

Her inspection ended at the museum, its front obscured by the mask of smoke and water. *My hopes going up in smoke.* A bitter laugh choked her, and she coughed. She shook her head and put her feet in action. *Move it, girl.* There must be something she could do to help. *Mitigate the losses.* A phrase from her father. *Salvage what you can and move on.* A thread of hope leaked into the fire in her head and she ran for the café door.

Inside, light contrasted with the night-dusk outside. The tables were shoved together in a horseshoe along the walls. Women carried plates, glasses and mugs from the kitchen. Pitchers of water followed. By the time Emily located Lenya, the first plate of sandwiches came through the door, carried by the red-headed teen from the ice cream stand. *Purpose, they all have a common purpose for a common good.*

Emily stumbled. *Purpose. What's my purpose? A heaviness she'd not felt before settled in her chest, pressing down on her heart. Survival, it's been self-survival for so long I have no purpose outside myself.* She regained solid footing, kicked aside the thought and headed toward Lenya.

Lenya did not question her arrival. "Emily, we could use more sandwich makers." She pointed to the swinging doors to the kitchen. "Devon will assign you." And she spun away.

Emily hung her jacket on a chair back and did as she was told. An inappropriate chuckle threatened to escape. Doing what she was told, without question, was a new experience. Moments later, after washing her hands, she stepped up to the production area. Devon slapped a knife in her hand, pointed at the butter dish and a stack of bread. And she was part of the line. *Part of the community, a contributing part.* A smile tweaked her mouth and a sense of well-being flowed through her. *Another new experience.*

The woman across from Emily, Marta from the grocery store, watched her and then lowered her gaze to handle her own task in the line. She hummed as she worked. Murmured conversation rose and fell in the room. Half sentences and references that Emily found vague, spoke to the familiarity of the people with each other. Emily ran out of bread and butter at the same time. She turned to ask for more and saw everyone putting their utensils in the sink.

Across from her, Marta nodded. "We have enough ready to feed an army," she said, her voice raspy. "We're done for now." She slid off her stool and took up her cane. "Let's go see what else needs doing."

Following Marta's lead, Emily joined the others in the main area. She eyed plates of sandwiches, pickles, cookies, and urns of soup and coffee, no, tea. Truly enough to feed an army. *Now I know what they mean when they say the table groaned under the load of food.*

The lull was short-lived. Hart burst through the doors, his face streaked black. "Come on," he said, waving an arm. "The fire has not hit the upstairs, and we want to keep it that way. We're going to remove as much material as we can to prevent water damage. Then they can flood things from above. Adults, head for the back fire escape." He shoved a box at Marta. "Make sure everyone gets a mask." And with that he disappeared and the front door banged shut behind him.

Marta position herself by the patio doors leading to the boardwalk and, as each woman headed out, handed them a plain dust mask. Not much coverage, but enough to ease the effect of the smoke that escaped the main funnel. Emily joined the line. Marta stared at her for a long moment with that half-knowing, half-questioning look she'd given Emily earlier, and handed over a mask.

No one complained, no one suggested another plan, no one said much of anything other than, *after you, let's go. So bloody polite even in a crisis.*

They headed through a darkness alive with dancing reflections of flames and, Emily sniffed, air coated with burning wood and damp smoke. Breaking into a steady, running pace, she followed the others toward the back of the museum. Hart, there ahead of them, stood beside a second uniformed volunteer. Devon kissed the man on the cheek and received a quick hug in return. *That must be her husband, Greg.*

A pump, sucking water out of the cove, provided an almost primal beat. Hart delivered instructions. "Greg and I will go inside and bring out the boxes. The rest of you please form a line up the stairs, and guide the containers as they slide down. Those left at the bottom can receive and, working in pairs, carry each tub to safety." He pointed. "The far side of the ice cream cart should be good. Everybody got it?"

Murmurs of agreement answered him, and Hart and Greg donned their breathing masks, switched on their air tanks and headed up the stairs and into the building. Under Lenya's direction, the women divided into teams.

She eyed Emily. "Emily, you look strong, how about you join the carrying line." And Emily did.

"Kelsey." Lenya's voice was sharp. "You are not to be near this process. Baby's safety comes first. Head over to the ice cream cart and direct the stacking." Kelsey opened her mouth and Lenya raised one finger and glared. Kelsey huffed and headed for her assigned station.

The men brought out the boxes, and Lenya slid them to the first step so the others could edge them down. The line functioned with only the occasional runaway box. By the fifth container, they had a process that matched the rhythm of the pump. Grip, slide, pass, repeat. At the end of the run, pairs of women hoisted the boxes and disappeared behind the ice cream stand. No rush, no panic, just the steady movement of material.

Emily, partnered with a woman she'd not met before, carried box after box to the growing stack. "This is a lot of material," she said on what must have been the twenty-fifth box.

They waited in the line for their next load. The woman scrunched her face. "Three hundred years of history, you know. Some of this is one-of-a-kind. I hope we save it."

"No kidding." Moisture and heat filled Emily's mask and smoke made her eyes water. She used her shirttail to wipe sweat off her neck. Rolling her shoulders, she stepped in beside the next container and once again carried irreplaceable materials to safety. A greater good. Not saving lives. Not creating a cure for cancer. But preserving histories, family stories and links through generations. Some folk dismissed the past. Emily had lived with no connections and, to her, saving histories mattered.

"And there are pictures," the woman added. "And other stuff. Not sure what all Lem has stashed in these things. But his museum and history tour bring a lot of business to the cove. People are just starting to move back and live here."

Finally, Hart stepped out on the upper landing and pulled off his mask and eye shield. He wiped the back of his hand over his forehead. "One more and we're done." He followed a box down the stairs. "I'll go tell the guys they can soak the second story."

Emily and her partner had the privilege of taking away the final box. The other women, followed by Greg, came down the steps and joined the rest by the saved materials. The last box was added to the rows already safely stored. The women pulled off their masks. Clapping and cheering broke out and hugs became the order of the moment.

Hart returned. "Good job, everyone. Now that they can soak the whole building, they can eliminate the fire." He frowned. "Then we can put them all back."

The women booed and several threw hats at him. Laughter rippled briefly through the group and pairs and trios gathered to talk. Emily leaned against the ice cream stand. The webbed connection joining these people was almost visible. Gwen glanced up and saw Emily. She marched over, linked her arm with Emily's and pulled her toward the rest of the Touched by Murder gals. "Come on, girlfriend."

Emily knew her face was grinning and an emotion she couldn't quite define infused her breathing and settled warm in her stomach like a bowl of tomato soup. Like the tomato soup her mother used to make. She had not felt this safe, or this connected, since those childhood days.

Bonus. You have found a bonus. Even if you can't find your biological family, you are being offered family here, in this group.

The long-seated desire to know her own roots argued—*close, but no cigar.* Her inner child was not ready to let go of hope yet. *There has to be a way to find the information. There has to be.*

If her beginnings were in this community, she wanted to be the first to know. She needed to have time to observe, to process, before stepping into and acknowledging her history. *Control freak.* Her girlfriends back in Ontario teased her about that. But they were right. She wanted control and the opportunity to see if she would be accepted.

Most of all, right now, she wanted water. The women moved back to the café and the volunteer firemen straggled in. They nodded, clapped each other on the back and drained glasses of water. Sandwiches disappeared followed by cookies and more water. Finally, Lem, Greg and Harvey entered the café. *When had Harvey arrived?*

"Is the fire out?"

"How much was damaged?"

"What caused the fire?"

"Was anyone hurt?"

Lem raised a hand. "Water first. Answers after." The crowd parted and the three men retrieved their well-deserved refreshments.

"Now," Lem said as he brushed crumbs off his jacket, "here's what we know. The fire appears to have started in the entry hall. The most damage is to the pictures and two family trees there as well as the lower part of the staircase. The workroom suffered smoke and water damage. Thanks to the box brigade and the plastic containers, most of the unsorted material should be safe."

"How do you think it started?"

Greg shook his head. "Jackson thinks maybe arson. We've put in a call and the investigators will be here at first light. Not much they can see tonight. We'll post a watch until they get here."

"Arson?"

"Who'd want to burn our museum?"

"Why'd they start a fire?"

"How did it start?"

"What did they hope to gain? It doesn't make sense."

A cold, damp chill flashed over Emily's skin. Sense? To her, it made horrible sense. Someone wanted to keep her family information from her. Or they wanted to have control of how and when she found out. She closed her eyes and fought back tears. This fire, this disaster in the family oriented community of Caleb's Cove was Dan's fault, her fault. Their history gave rise to the reason for the fire. People could have been hurt, killed even. Her search had endangered the families in Caleb's Cove. She and Dan should have stayed away—far, far away. When the truth came out, and it would sooner or later, they'd be a lot less friendly. Wouldn't they?

CHAPTER 14

Emily admired the efficiency of the community. The fire was out, the investigation team set to arrive in the morning and Lenya and Lem were spearheading discussions and plans for the cleanup. *The two of them are the instigators and fixers.* A pervasive reluctance to leave the security and comfort of the group prevailed. Two men left to relieve the guard duty at the museum and a draft of cool air swept over Emily. She shuddered, aware of the exhaustion rapidly overtaking her.

All she needed was her jacket. She checked a few chair backs, sure she'd put it on one of them. It wasn't there. In the kitchen? She might have been mistaken about the chair. She threaded through the crowd, smiling at those she knew. She found her jacket on the hooks behind the swinging door. Someone must have hung it up for her.

Once she had it on, she checked her pockets. Her wallet was in the left one and the keys—the keys were not in the right pocket. She scrabbled her fingers around the pocket, checked the left one and looked down. The breast pocket stuck out at an unusual angle. She poked in her fingers. They touched metal and she pulled out the keys.

She tossed them once, caught them in her hand and clenched her fingers around them. She never put her keys in that pocket. The damn thing stuck out far enough over her breast without being stuffed with keys. *Maybe they fell out and someone put them back in the wrong pocket. Maybe?* She closed her eyes and swayed with threatening sleep. *That must be it.*

The door swung open, and Lenya poked her head in. "I'm ready to head back if you are," she said.

Emily put the offending keys in the correct pocket and followed Lenya out. "No argument from me on that plan."

The moon had almost reached full height in the dark sky. In twos and threes, people trickled away home. Lenya's shoulders sagged and her footsteps dragged as she and Emily headed for the car. During the short drive, Emily descended into sleep, only to have her head loll to the side and jerk her awake. Outside, clouds now obliterated the stars and small gaps allowed shafts of moonlight to pierce the pools of shadow. Inside Lenya's car, only dash lights interrupted the dark and probed the inner darkness residing inside Emily.

Lenya pulled up by Emily's trailer. "There you go, dear. Thanks for your help. Sleep well."

Emily pulled the handle, cracking open the door. The overhead light illuminated Lenya and her yawn. "I was happy to help. But it seems like you'd have all done just fine even without me."

Lenya nodded. "Perhaps, but in an emergency every minute counts and every pair of hands helps."

Emily left the car and, hands jammed in her jacket pockets, headed to the trailer. Exhaustion cloaked the evening's events and created dead space in her mind. Getting into bed was the only thought in her head. But washing off the grime roused her, and once in her night clothes, restlessness stirred her muscles. She pulled out a mug and reached for her hot chocolate. *Not there. Right. Harvey took it for testing.*

She opened the fridge door and stood without comprehending. Her knees buckled, and she jerked awake. Milk—hot milk—would do. Whether it was the hot milk or simply the passage of time she was soon so weary she barely made it to the bed. Curled under her blanket, she dropped into immediate sleep.

Twinkle, twinkle little star.

The words accompanied by a tinkling tune drifted around her, and she struggled to wake. Who was playing the music? She rolled over and it was gone.

"Suzie, Suzie come and play with me." The high, girlish voice echoed in her dreams. Once again, almost awake, she sought the source before dropping back to sleep.

"Twinkle, twinkle little star." The music box. She turned, stretched out a hand but it was gone. Another room, another burst of music. Again she saw the white and pink box with its dancing ballerina and headed for it only to find it vanished.

As had happened the night before, she was aware of the

dreaming state and yet unable to break free and wake up. Time and again, she was roused by bursts of familiar music and names and voices that echoed weirdly familiar in her head. Time and again, she tossed, turned and attempted to find the source only to drop back into a restless, relentless sleep. Cool darkness faded and light filtered through the blinds. But still her brain refused to wake. Again she heard music. And again voices.

Farewell to Nova Scotia, the sea-bound coast.... The phrase, sung by a husky, female voice played on in some insidious loop.

Wake up. I need to wake. Movement should wake her. She kicked her feet, pulled her arms from under the blankets and, holding her hands up in the air, she fluttered them. Brief lucidity allowed her to realize she had only dreamed the movements. Heavy sleep dragged her under again.

Heat filled the trailer and voices echoed in the campground and, in one final, jerky movement, Emily sat up. Her hair straggled around her head and strands clung to her cheeks. Her shoulders ached and her P.J. collar, damp and clammy, clung to her. Her mouth was once again that telltale dryness that followed being drugged. Pounding filled her head and tightened her scalp. *What a night.*

Her tongue stuck to the roof of her mouth. She swallowed and triggered a bout of coughing. *Juice, I need some juice.* The frog episode popped into her thoughts, and she peered at the floor. *Nothing. Safe to step out.*

Shuffling steps took her to the fridge, and she drank straight from the carton. Backing up, she sank down at the kitchen table and slugged back more juice. She ran her tongue over her teeth, licked her lips and finished the juice. Limb by limb, organ by organ her body came awake.

The outside world intruded, and she checked the clock. Almost noon. Heavens, she'd slept for hours. She should be alert, but the grogginess refused to release its hold. It not only refused to leave, it seduced her toward more sleep.

I've never been this drowsy.

Yes, you have. After the wedding.

All connected? I must have been drugged both times. How, when, by whom?

This time it had to be the milk.

In spite of a hot shower and three mugs of black coffee, she couldn't shake the fuzziness in her brain. Every time she stopped moving, her brain, if not her body, slid into a state of suspended animation. She secured the door, locked her shoulder bag in the truck and went behind the trailer. She stared at her bike. *No, not a good idea, I'd probably fall into a ditch.*

She checked that her keys were in the correct pocket and headed toward the beach. A brisk breeze swept over her as she stepped out of the shelter of the trees. *Just what I need—a clean wind and a rousing walk.*

. . . . .

Emily walked for hours, heading away from the cove and finding the docks and boathouses of summer homes along the shore. By the time she returned, the sun hung low in the western sky, and the sea air hung damply over the beach. She paced up the tree-shaded path and reached her door. The brain cobwebs had been swept away and replaced with weariness. She could only hope that a good night's sleep lay ahead. Three nights of tossing and turning and dreams was quite enough.

Inserting her key in each lock in turn, she pulled open the door. Stepping up, she fumbled for the light switch to banish the interior dimness. Warm air drifted out of the trailer, brushed her face and dissipated into the cooler night.

The overhead light assaulted her vision and she blinked. She hung her keys on the hook and turned to head toward the small kitchen. Her feet stumbled. Her eyes blinked. Clutter stretched along the short, center area. What the…? She shook her head but the action did not dispel the mess. She stepped in, finding spots for her feet between the scattered papers, the slashed cushions and the drawers tossed on top.

Had her watcher done this? Did he think he could scare her? Disbelief gave way to growing anger. How was this slimy, sneaky son of a hound getting in? Especially without being seen? Logic told her the door faced the path and field and that other campers couldn't see the door, unless they were out walking. She stomped out of the trailer and across the gravel to the canteen. Letting the door bang behind her, she confronted Lenya.

"Did you see anyone go into my trailer?"

Lenya took one step back. "What? No? But I can't really see the door from here."

"Damn." Emily sagged against the counter and her anger settled. She couldn't let this go on. There had to be a way to end it.

Lenya came around the counter and put both hands on Emily's shoulders. "What happened?"

"Someone was in my trailer, again." Emily pressed her lips together. "They trashed the place."

"We should call Harvey."

Emily shook her head. "Not now. I should clean up." She half-turned toward the door.

"No, that's the last thing you should do. Don't you watch cop shows?" Lenya's voice was kind. "Let me call Harvey and get you a cup of tea."

"Yes. No." Emily rubbed her hands on her upper arms. "I should at least go and lock the trailer."

"Fair enough. I'll call Harvey and put the kettle on," Lenya said.

Emily turned and, at a half-run, was out the door. She stepped into the trailer and stared at the wreckage. Calming her mind and stilling her breath, she ran a gaze from one end to the other. Was anything missing?

She stepped over the bench cushions where they lay on the floor and checked the bed area. One hand on the edge of the bed, she looked back. Her frog, the stuffed one, was missing. Her gaze snapped to the cabinet under the sink. Thank goodness they had not found the safe. Or had they? *Maybe they tidied it up so you wouldn't know.*

Going to the sink, she knelt down and with her sleeve over her fingers, lifted the floor boards. *There, I do watch TV police dramas.* Opening the safe, she reached in for her pictures and wallet. They were still there. A quick scoop around with her hand and she found the jewelry box with the necklace. They were all safe. But should she put them back? She chewed on her lip. Yes. They were still safer there than anywhere else.

She locked the safe, replaced the cabinet floor and stood. With her back against the counter, she examined her disrupted space from that angle. A slip of white protruded from the near side of a displaced cushion. She knelt and pulled on the folded sheet of paper. She opened it and black, block letters stared up her, just like the letters on that brown paper. She slid to the floor, her back supported by the cabinets.

I know who you are. Do not call the police.
Well too late for that instruction. Lenya had probably called Harvey by now.

Help me find the money and I'll tell you everything I know.
Too bad, buddy, but I don't know where to find the money.

Did you like my fireworks? If that didn't convince you to see me, I can arrange a sinking of a boat, an explosion in the café kitchen—or worse. Things are set up, all I need to do is push a button.

Damn, I can't let him cause any more harm. What if he kills someone?

I'll be in the trees at the south side of the grocery store - be there - no later than an hour after dark or ka-boom.

Why on earth did he chose that spot? The store would be closed, but it was on the main drag.

And come alone….The final words resonated in her skull.
Alone? I usually go everywhere alone.

The nasty, dirty son of a….Who the heck did he think he was? Emily saw red and crumpled the note and let it fly overhand under the table. She punched the pillows that had been so unceremoniously dumped on the floor. Struggling to her feet, she clutched her keys until her palm hurt. *Enough already.*

For about thirty seconds she told herself that she should look at the situation logically. She should tell the police, wait for Harvey and let him handle it. But the thirty seconds passed. She looked at the clock and glanced out the window. The sun had traveled below the trees and buildings. Darkness was imminent.

My life, my decision, my risk. Ka-boom? He'll do it. Unless I can stop him.

She switched off the lights, remembered the note and retrieving it, stuff it in her purse. The hand-lock locked behind her, and she twisted the key in the deadbolt. In the truck, she shoved her purse under the seat. Cranking the engine, she put it in gear. As she stomped on the gas, a wave of surreal fear washed over her. She had no idea what Dan had done with the money. Could she trick the threatening idiot into believing she did? If not, the game was over and done and she might be dead.

CHAPTER 15

The man waited for his prey leaning back against a tree. The hanging branches obscured part of his view, but he didn't mind because it also hid him from passers. She'd either come or not. Had he dangled enough of a temptation? Enough of a threat? He glanced at his watch. She'd better come soon or he would not be able to get into the cave. He had to be in and out before high tide.

 A car passed on the road. It was the only one that had gone by in at least fifteen minutes. The café closed at eight this evening and soon even the staff would be gone. The tourists would be chowing down on seafood in either Lunenburg or Bridgewater. The campers, seated around their fire pits, would have donned jackets to ward off the damp as the seaward winds shifted and headed inland.

 He fingered the tube in his pocket. The syringe was filled and ready to go. He had considered the dose carefully. He needed her under while he carried out the snatch, but wanted her at least semi-coherent as he deposited her in the cave. He allowed his laugh to gurgle in his chest. He knew the closed space would freak her out and he wanted to see it happen.

 Another vehicle approached from the north. He raised a hand and pushed aside the branch directly in front of him. A truck. Hers? He waited. In moments the truck turned off the road and drew into the parking area. Yes. He punched his fists one after the other into the air. *She is here. Now the fun begins.*

 The truck made a U-turn and his euphoria hiccupped. What was she up to? Afraid she'd leave, he almost blew his cover. But in moments, she backed up the drive alongside the building. He had to admire her caution. She was ready to bolt if she had to. Additionally, she did not turn off the engine. He waited. She leaned toward the windshield with her forearms wrapped around the top of the steering wheel. A look to the parking lot was followed by an inspection in his direction. Did she see him? He'd like to leave her wait longer, but time was passing.

He stepped out from under his leafy cover and headed for the passenger door now conveniently located close to him. He tried the door. Locked. One careful young lady. He paused, met her wide-eyed gaze and saw a young woman. Not the girl, not the kid with the pigtails and teeth missing. Not the child who had been fascinated when he sang with her parents. He knocked on the window and held up his cell phone. He positioned his thumb as if to press one number. "Your choice."

She sat back quickly, jerky movements giving away her fright. At least he hoped it was fright. She turned a flashlight in his direction, and he allowed her to get a good look at his face. She wouldn't live long enough to identify him. He smiled, tilted his head in greeting. It was all he could do to look benign when he wanted to bare his teeth, roar at her and wrap his hands around her neck. Shake the information out of her. She focused on the cell phone and unlocked the door.

"It's okay, Suzie-Q, I just want to talk." He pulled the handle. The overhead light came on and he shifted onto the seat and closed the door. Too much light might attract attention. From whom he wasn't sure, since the closet person had already been dealt with. But you never knew who was roaming around in this place.

"Who are you?" she demanded.

He made her wait. Control of this interview was his. Not hers.

"Don't you remember me?" he asked. "You used to call me Uncle Phil." He reached out to stroke her cheek and she jerked away.

She frowned, chewed her lip obviously trying to remember. In the end, she shook her head.

"Never mind. I've changed a lot since the days I used to work the bars with Lily."

She started and her eyes went wider.

"Yes," he said, "your momma was a bar singer, a damn good one at that. If everything had not gone sideways, she might have been a big name like that Twain gal." And Lily had been good, her whiskey voice charming the audience. His job had been to accompany her on the guitar. But she didn't really need him. He growled. Enough. This was not about his memories, it was about her memories and information he needed to find the rest of the loot.

"You said you could tell me my history?" Her voice, demanding and sharp, cut through his reminiscing.

"That was a conditional offer. You need to give me something in exchange, and you get to go first." He leered at her and put his hand into the pocket with the syringe.

"I have fifty thousand of the money. You can have it all."

"That's a paltry portion of almost two million dollars. I want what Dan took."

"Dan had a package made up," she said. "With information for me."

"And?"

"He said he'd bring it to me, but that was the night he was killed. I didn't get it. If we can find that package, we'll have what you want. Since the police are still digging around, I don't think they found it." There was no hesitation in her words, no shakiness in her voice. She believed what she was saying.

"You think it's somewhere here in Caleb Cove?"

"I do. If we combine forces, I think we can find it. You can have the money. All I want is my history."

"Fair enough," he said. Let her think he planned to cooperate. Build her up and then pull the rug out from under her. "You saw your mother's grave today?"

She nodded.

"That's your starting point. She grew up here." He paused, savoring the expectant look on her face, the longing in her eyes. "When we find the package, I'll tell you her last name." *Right before you die.*

Suzie-Q deflated physically and her breath whooshed out. But she rallied. "Have you been piping music into my trailer at night?"

"Smart girl."

"My mother used to sing Farewell to Nova Scotia to me, didn't she?"

He shrugged. No harm in her knowing that. "Sure did. It was her signature song. She'd finish every gig with it."

"Where did you put the drugs? In my milk?"

He laughed. She really was one smart cookie.

"Who is Becky?"

He stiffened. "Don't you say her name. She was your friend and you left her. You and that precious father of yours." This conversation was over.

Using his thumb, he pushed the cap off the needle. "Don't worry, Suzie-Q, you'll find out everything you need to know." He removed his hand from the pocket, palming the syringe. He extend the hand toward her and, when she pulled back, leaned toward her bringing his free hand to cup her face. Before she could react further, he plunged the needle into her neck and pushed in the plunger.

Her eyebrows rose, her mouth formed in an O and her nostrils flared. Shocked was she? And maybe, just maybe, fearful. Satisfaction pooled in his belly. This dominance over her was worth more than the money. Especially since he wouldn't get to keep the money. His cousin might not be happy if he didn't get his money, but right now Phil didn't care.

Her hand came up to grab his, and she pushed against the offending arm without effect. The drug was already working. He laughed and pulled the needle from her neck. "You are mine now, Suzie Q, and we'll have a chat soon about the sins of your father."

The fear in her eyes was unmistakable. As her eyelids drifted closed and her body slumped, he turned away, recapped the needle and put it back in his pocket. He rubbed his hands briskly together. Now he needed to get busy.

He'd transfer her to his van and return her truck to the campsite. After placing her purse inside the trailer, and leaving it unlocked, he'd return on her bicycle. After all, he had the keys to the locks. Step two—drive the van to the beach, get her into the rowboat and off to the cave. He sighed in satisfaction and reached over to pull her toward the passenger seat. It sure was nice when a plan came together.

. . . . .

Harvey thumbed his phone's on-button. "Conrad here."
"Harvey, it's Lenya. Someone trashed Emily's trailer."
Harvey sat up, planted his feet on the floor and turned off the TV. Frogs were one thing—a prank. Break and enter, bugging the place and destroying property was something else altogether.
"When did this happen?" *Ms. Martin knows something, has seen something tied to Dan Grady's death. It is too much of a coincidence. Why isn't she talking?*

"I think this afternoon. I saw her head out for a walk early afternoon. It was almost dusk when she came rushing in here. It must have happened somewhere in there. She sure was upset."

This had to be connected to the murder. "I'm on my way," he said and rang off. He collected Turner and headed for the cove.

"Basically," he said to Turner as they headed down the 331, "these are the reasons why I think she's connected. First, she found the body. Why had she gone into a stranger's in the first place?

"Second, her fingerprints were all over the camper, not just around the body. She eats those power bars too, and a wrapper of the same type was found under the table. Third, she was in there for over twenty minutes before exiting and reporting the death.

"Fourth, someone has been harassing her since the murder. And last, but not least, my gut is telling me that she is hiding something."

Turner grunted in assent.

He and Turner had no further exchanges as he concentrated on keeping the pedal down and the car on the road. He parked at the canteen and headed inside.

Lenya came toward them, her brow furrowed and her mouth tight. "I don't understand," she said. "Emily came and talked to me. We agreed to call you and wait. She went to lock up, and I went back to the kitchen to make a real cup of tea." She threw out both hands. "When I came out, her truck was tearing up the exit road."

Dave Lamont stood by, feet spread and shoulders squared. How did he figure in all of this?

Harvey looked at Turner. Turner went out on the porch. He returned, shaking his head.

"So, it's still gone?"

Turner took a breath, paused. "Truck is there."

"What? I didn't hear it come back and I had the main door open just in case." Lenya went to the door and looked for herself.

Dave followed her. "It wasn't there when I came over to see Lenya. She must have come back later."

"Did you leave the front area at all?" Harvey asked, including both Lenya and Dave in his look.

"Darn. Yes, I went to the storeroom for chocolate bars." Lenya looked at Dave. "Dave came to help me carry boxes. Thought I might as well stock the shelves while I waited. It's better to keep busy instead of worrying. She said she was coming back for the tea."

Lenya sank onto a stool.

Harvey expelled a deep breath. "Ah well, come on, let's go take a look."

He led the way to the trailer, fully expecting to find the independent Ms. Martin keeping watch over her trashed goods. He'd noticed her independent streak earlier. But there were no lights and no one answered when he knocked. The others stood about two feet behind him. Turner straight and stoic, Lenya looking worried, and Dave Lamont hanging back.

Harvey knocked again. Waited. Nothing.

He motioned for Turner to get Lenya and Dave away from the trailer. Once they were at a safe distance, Turner returned and they both unsnapped their holsters.

"Ms. Martin," Harvey called out. "It's Constable Conrad. Are you in there?" Silence settled around them and even the night sounds of the trees and scurrying animals seemed to cease. He turned the doorknob and found it unlocked. His heartrate escalated.

"We're coming in." Harvey took the two steps up and entered the trailer. Heat and silence greeted him. He glanced back at Turner who nodded. Harvey braced as Turner flipped on the lights. The mess that greeted him was complete. But no human, alive or dead, peopled the trailer. He could see from one end to the other, and unless she was stuffed into the tiny washroom, the place was empty. He took a full scan around. Her purse was on the table and her computer in the sink. No keys in sight.

He opened the washroom door, just in case. "No one here. Get the camera," he said to Turner. His partner strode off toward the squad car.

Lenya came to the door. "How can her truck be here and she's gone? She was pretty shook up and, at this time of night, I can't think she went off for a stroll on the beach."

"We'll check," Harvey said. He pulled out his phone. "In the meantime, we could use a few more eyes on the ground."

Lenya turned on her heel. "I know where we can get help faster than waiting for people from Bridgewater." She was gone, heading back to the canteen before Harvey could stop her.

He shook his head and requested backup of a police kind. These darn people in Caleb's Cove were always taking things into their own hands. And he'd learned there was no way to stop them. He finished his call to the detachment and called Natalie Parker. Filling her in on things, he asked her to get downstairs to the café and ride herd on the locals. He knew damn well they'd congregate there.

Harvey pulled out his gloves and started a foot-by-foot inspection of the small space that was Emily Martin's home-on-the-road. Maybe he'd find something new or different from his previous search, something that would point him in Emily's direction.

CHAPTER 16

Emily's stomach sloshed, her tongue stuck to the roof of her mouth. *Stop the rocking, please. Stop or I'll puke.* The words bounced in her head and the rocking continued. *Why didn't it stop?*

The point in her neck where the needle had gone in burned. *He drugged me.*

She struggled, lost the fight and slid back under the curtain of darkness. A bump propelled her back to consciousness. Hands grabbed her.

"Come on, get your butt up and out of there." His voice. *Now he has a name. Phil.*

She sat up, half by herself, half pulled by his hands and opened her eyes. Only a narrow beam of light pierced the black. Her head drooped. Hands gripped her again, dragging her this time, and she followed the direction of the pulling, scrabbling her feet to keep up with her body. She landed on her side against an even harder, lumpier surface. Her legs scraped over a barrier and both feet splashed into the water. Cold, hard and sharp, the surface under her dug into her face.

A grunt accompanied the next tug and she moved forward, got her feet out of water and lay there. *Why can't I focus?* Her brain slid under again. The hands shook her.

A phone rang and the shaking stopped. "You need it checked when...okay, okay, I'll be there." *His, Phil's, voice again. And he has the tattoo.*

"Wake up there, Suzie-Q. You need to hear this. I'm leaving you. I don't have time to get what I want before the tide locks the entrance. And I have errands to tend to. Don't fall back the way you came in or you may drown, and we can't have that, at least, not yet." His laugh rose around her, hollow and dead. "I'll be back when the tide goes down." A hand slapped her face twice. "Hear me?"

She managed a strangled answer. "Yes." She wanted to laugh or maybe it was she wanted to cry. She had nothing to tell him. He could come back if he liked, but it would do no good. Her brain fired on enough synapses to tell her she was dead one way or the other. *Unless you save yourself.* On that whisper from her sub-conscience, she floated into deep sleep once more.

I have to pee. She put her hand up and banged her knuckles. *I can't get out. But I really have to pee.* Tears leaked out of her eyes. She pulled her knees up to her chest and curled her arms around them.

I can't pee my pants. I'm a big girl. Mommy, come and get me out.

Memory overwhelmed her. Remembered warmth ran down her leg and shame washed over her. *Mommy, why didn't you come?*

I'm dreaming. I must be dreaming. I remember! I was five and hiding in the window box. Mommy said I needed to stay until she came.

The substance of her recurring nightmare washed over her, finally remembered. *Mommy never came. I was there a long time and then Daddy came. But he wasn't mad at me for peeing my pants. He got me dry clothing, and I took my frog and dolly and we left. He said Mommy had gone to heaven.*

Emily put her hand up again. She stubbed her fingers against hard rock. *Where am I now? I am not five years old.* Her mind screamed, and she jerked, trying to sit. Her backside suffered hard pokes and her head connected at the top. Pain knifed along her scalp, and a warm trickle ran down her forehead. She put both hands over her face and her mind screamed again. Long, agonizing sounds that refused to push past the lock-hold fear had on her throat.

Her breath came in short, panicked puffs. Her heart raced and her muscles tensed. But she could go nowhere. The space was too small. And the ocean rose steadily, lapping once again at her feet. Would it fill the cavity and drown her? Weeping, she curled into a ball with her arms over her head. Her worst nightmare come true.

. . . . .

Harvey worked his way from the bed area, past the tiny washroom and the equally compact kitchen. Across from the sink and counter, he checked the table. Meanwhile, Turner dumped out Emily's purse and sorted through her belongings.

"Harvey." Turner's voice left no doubt that what he had found was serious. He handed over the smoothed-out paper.

Harvey read quickly, not sure what the first part referred to, but absolutely certain what the rest meant. Emily Martin had gone to meet her stalker. And if the man had really started that fire, he was way more dangerous than Harvey had suspected. Swear words reserved for moments like this swarmed in his mind and threatened to spill out. Clamping down on them he turned.

"Come on, Turner. Time to move." He pushed the other officer out the door and followed, taking over the lead as they ran for the squad car. He took the wheel, way too edgy to sit and be driven by Turner.

He shoved the note at Turner. "Bag that," Harvey ordered. "And call and find out the ETA of our back-up." He shoved the gear stick into drive and the car jumped ahead. Flooring the gas, Harvey tore out of the campground. *Darn, crazy, incautious woman. With a murderer on the loose, how dare she go off to meet someone she did not know?*

"Fifteen minutes," Turner said. "It'll take them that long even with lights and siren."

Fifteen minutes was too damn long. He was not going to wait. "Brace yourself," he said to Turner and pushed the car even faster. They swung around the corner onto the main road and raced for the center of Caleb Cove and the grocery store.

He passed the café with its lights blazing, and slowed enough to make a decent turn into the store parking lot. Leaving the lights on, he leaned forward and swept his inspection across the lot and as far as he could see up the sides of the building. Nothing. Too dark and too many trees.

"Let's go," he said to Turner and, switching on his flashlight, he exited the car. Turner paralleled his moves. Only feet apart they walked the lot, approached the store and worked across the front. At the south side, Harvey stopped and shone his light on the ground. "Tire marks," he muttered and swept the light beam back and forth. Along the side of the treads, he saw something more. "Drag marks."

"And partial footprints," Turner added. "They look like boot prints. The heels are dug in like he was carrying something heavy." He placed his foot beside a nearly full print. "Has to be at least a size 10, maybe 12, like mine." He pointed closer to the tree line. "And there is another set of tire treads."

Both of them squatted and examined the lines. Careful not to disturb the prints, they worked their way up the side of the building.

"More tire marks," Turner said. "Not the same tread as the main ones. More like the set closer to the trees. The drag marks end here and the footprints in this semi-circle are less indented."

"What's your assessment," Harvey asked, "taking into account what we see here and what was in the note."

"Someone or something was removed from the vehicle back there." Turner pointed, "Whatever it was, was dragged up here and placed in the second vehicle. Given the note, it was probably the stalker's vehicle. The person doing the dragging then went around here and headed back, keeping close to the trees." He checked the ground at the end of the first tracks and followed them toward the road.

"He came out of the trees here, went around the vehicle and got into this side of the truck." Turner pointed to the south side. "I'd say, looking at the faint marks over here by the gravel, that this vehicle was backed into place." He walked to the far side of the first tire marks. "Looks like the person got into the truck, if it was indeed Martin's truck."

Harvey sighed. His assessment exactly. *The stalker had snatched Emily, driven her truck back to the campground and returned somehow, before driving away with her.* He walked further back along the building. Crushed bushes caught his eye. He shone the light on them and parted some branches. Ms. Emily Martin's bicycle lay where it had been tossed. *Not good, not good at all.*

Turner looked toward the store. "Doesn't the owner live up there?" He pointed to the third floor of the building.

Of course she does. "I'll go see if she's there. You take a quick check in her garage and then join me. I'll wait at the front." There were no lights in the main level, but Harvey headed for the entrance anyway. *Leave no stone unturned, or no door unchecked.* He pulled on the door and stepped back in a hurry when it swung toward him. Unsnapping his gun holster, he raised his flashlight in front of him and waited. As soon as he felt Turner behind him, he started into the store.

"Police," he called. "We're coming in."

Three steps inside, he found a display of cereal boxes strewn across the floor. His adrenaline levels spiked and every fiber in his body went on alert. He edged past the boxes, scanning as he went.

Turner went to the aisle along the far wall and matched Harvey's trip to the back of the store.

"Clear." Turner's voice arched and fell in the dark store.

Harvey finished the main aisle and the coffee corner and matched his call. "Clear." He swung open the door to the office and swept the light around the room. The deck chair was shoved back against the far wall, and a sheaf of papers splayed across the floor. "Clear," he called. "But it looks like someone left in a hurry."

Turner joined Harvey. "There is a car in the garage."

They headed to the staircase and edged up the stairs, but saw no one, heard nothing. An inspection of the second floor storage area yielded nothing more than boxes and display stands. At the third floor landing, Harvey knocked on the apartment door and called out. "Police. Marta? Are you there?"

No answer. He turned the doorknob, and the door swung open on a dark room. Someone had been leaving a lot of doors unlocked. The sweep showed nothing but a package of ground chicken thawing on the counter. Marta hadn't arrived to make her supper. She was not there at all. Harvey stuck the chicken in the fridge. "Just in case finding her takes a long time."

Lights swept the front windows. Two vehicles. Reinforcements. Harvey led the way down and greeted the officers with a grim look. "Cordon off," he said, and filled them in on what had been found. "As soon as you can, free up a couple of you to help with the search."

"It's an island," one of the newly arrived officers said, "how hard can it be to find them?"

Harvey fixed a stare on the rookie. "Wooded areas, convoluted coastline, caves, coves and nooks and crannies. Not to mention boats. You do know what boats are for?" The rookie's ears turned red. He'd learn.

"Come on, Turner," Harvey said. "Let's go see how Parker is making out with the locals. If they are hell-bent on helping, we might as well get them organized." Turner took the wheel and they headed for the café. It was going to be a long night.

CHAPTER 17

The minute they stepped into the café, they were surrounded by women. Lenya, Devon Ritcey and Kelsey Maxwell. Hart stood behind them, his curiosity evident on his face. And at the far end of the room, Gwen was on the phone. Natalie Parker leaned over a table, paper in front of her and a pen in her hand. She turned at the commotion and grinned at Harvey.

He shot her a dirty look and held up a hand. "Take it easy." He walked past the women and headed for Parker. "What's up?" They both spoke at the same time.

He looked at the attentive group, made an executive decision, and started. "Looks like Emily Martin went to the store to meet someone and left with them." He kept the details to himself. "Marta is not there right now, so we can't ask her if she saw anything."

"Ha!" Devon moved front and center and stared at Harvey. "What are you not telling us? We saw the extra police cars go past. You wouldn't call them just because Emily and Marta had gone somewhere else."

Turner guffawed.

Harvey held up a finger and pointed at him before turning his attention back to Devon. "Okay. It looks like they did not go of their own choice."

"I knew it. In other words, they were snatched." Devon's voice held satisfaction and a certain disturbing relish. Nanoseconds later, her brows dipped and her mouth turned down at the corners. "Not good, eh?"

Harvey tilted his head in acknowledgment. No more words needed.

"All right then." Kelsey stepped into the fray. "Let's get with it. There has to be a search of course, but the more eyes on the case the better." She turned to where Gwen had just hung up the phone.

"What did you find out?"

Gwen joined them. "I've got Auntie running a phone tree. If anyone has seen anything, we'll know soon enough. Her report is that she saw a couple of local cars go by, and a white van go up, about eight-thirty. It came back down quite a bit later. She was just about to head to bed. So she estimates around ten, maybe ten-thirty."

Harvey looked at his watch. Almost midnight. Anything could have happened since ten. And the way it was phrased, the white van was not local. "Do we know who owns the van?"

Hart spoke up. "I think it belongs to a man staying in Enos Oickle's place. He's come here a couple of times. Likes licorice ice cream."

Harvey's antennae quivered. Oickle. An unusual name that he'd heard recently.

"And he was on the tour earlier today. At least he left here with the tourists." Gwen added her bit. "Any time he came in, and it wasn't that often, he paid in cash. That much I remember."

Lenya raised a finger and, as if shaking it would help her remember, she shook it. "Enos died, let me see. Has to be about eighteen months ago. I heard he left the place to a relative. As far as I know, there are only two. One is a son and the other his nephew. They both came here for a couple summers back years ago. They would have been in their late teens. Seems to me they were a bit, um, wild? One of them ended up in jail, I think."

Harvey's interest ran up a red flag. One of the fingerprints in Dan's trailer had belonged to a convicted felon. He'd been out for about four years, and the system had lost track of him. They'd got the main details by email. A theft of cash, over a million worth, had been executed in Montreal. One man was killed, one arrested and one got away. "Do you know their names?"

"Um, the son was Ray, I think. And the other one, Phil, Bill? Not sure. His last same wasn't Oickle either. His mother was Enos's sister."

"Phil Doucette, maybe?"

"Could be."

Dave Lamont stepped up. "I know it was Phil Doucette."

Harvey shot him a sharp glance. "How do you know?"

"I was a rookie cop when that theft took place. I was first officer on the scene of the car crash. Doucette was stuck in the car and we arrested him. I've never forgotten the case. It was my first really big one. I knew Doucette had an uncle here, that's why I'm here. I figured he might show up. If there was any way he connected with Jones, the one that got away, I wanted to know. There would be money to recover."

Harvey felt the spike of a headache starting behind his left ear. This was getting more complicated by the minute. He turned to Turner. "Get on the phone. Get us a warrant to search this Doucette's place. With his fingerprint at a murder scene and his proximity to the disappearance of two women, we should get one easily."

Had Dan been somehow connected to this Phil person? Was the money from their heist the money is question? And what the bloody hell did Emily, a generation younger, have to do with it all?

Turner headed to the front of the café, pulling out his phone as he went.

"One other thing," Lenya said. "Bobby Jones married auntie's daughter. A few years later, we got the call that she'd been killed in Montreal."

"I remember that," Dave Lamont said. "It was a nasty deal."

The headache spike behind Harvey's ear flattened to playing card size. *Damn, I don't need a headache.* "Okay who is this auntie you and Gwen referred to?"

"My aunt and Gwen's great aunt, Mrs. Esther Gerber."

I should have guessed there were more relatives in the bushes.

Harvey pointed to Turner. "Make notes to follow up on Doucette and Jones." To Lamont he said, "You stay close, I'm going to want to talk to you once we find her." He turned to Parker. "Please tell me that's a map you have over there."

"Sure is." Parker turned to the map. "It's one of Lem's so it has everyone's house, the boat launches, the graveyard—everything you need to know."

Turner joined her and looked down at the map. "Okay, where exactly is this Enos Oickle's property?" Sounded like that place and the man, Phil Doucette, were their best bets.

Harvey scanned the digital copy of the warrant Turner had finessed. The authorities had decreed an ex-con and two missing women provided sufficient reasons to search. The detachment had dispatched the original warrant by squad car. Harvey joined Turner in the car and summoned two of the officers from the store. The more eyes the better.

Heading for the house on the cliff, the officers progressed silently with no warning sirens or flashing lights. They edged into the drive. Darkness shrouded the small home. The men left the cars. A cursory examination of the yard and lawn beyond did not find the white van. And there were no outbuildings.

"Let's go." Harvey pulled his gun and readied his flashlights. The others followed his lead. "You two," Harvey said, gesturing at the extra men, "take the back door. Turner—with me."

Harvey tried the door handle and found it locked. He knocked on the door. "Police officers," he called and knocked again. There was no response. "We are coming in," he yelled, and put his shoulder to the door. The building was old, the wood dry and the door frame split and gave access with one shove.

Harvey turned left into a small kitchen. Turner went right through the living room. "Clear," Turner called and Harvey echoed the response. They flipped on the living room lights and checked the two remaining doors.

"Pantry here," Turner called.

"Washroom." Harvey closed the door and he and Turner headed down the hall toward doors that probably led to bedrooms.

Turner stepped through the first door and flipped on the overhead light. "Hey, Harv," he yelled. "You gotta see this."

The other men joined Harvey and, moving into the room, they stared at each wall in turn.

Harvey pulled on gloves and stepped up to the wall on the right. Photographs of Caleb's Cove and area, including numerous coves and shorelines, plastered the space. Various residents appeared in one photo or another. Tapping with one finger, Harvey counted. "Eight of these are of Marta." Why was this guy so interested in her?

"Campground photos on this side," Turner said.

Harvey joined him. The whole wall was covered with photos of the campground. Shots of Dan Grady's unit from all sides formed a square. Another cluster showed photographs of Emily Martin, including one of her washing her hair in the shower. A full frontal picture of her had a large red X through it.

"Holy crap." The rookie expressed what they were all thinking. This guy was a serious stalker.

"Camera," Harvey said, and the rookie went out.

Moving closer to the third wall, Harvey peered at tide representations, current flows, high and low tide charts and photos of cliff areas, caves and small curved beaches. Pairs of pictures showed the same areas at both high and low tide. "This guy did some serious research."

"These were taken from a cliff or beach area at night. Look at that vista. It covers a full 180 around the areas. Checking for lights? Sea traffic?" Harvey shook his head. "This is about more than snatching the two women."

He dialed Parker. "I think I found your connection," he said. "You're going to want to come over here, believe me." He turned from that wall and looked back at pictures of the women.

Turner was bent over, peering at a small photo on the edge of the collage. "Come see," he said and looked back at Harvey.

The photo, a black and white shot, showed four young people grinning at the camera. Given the outfits they were wearing, the picture was most likely taken in the eighties. Three men and a woman—a girl really. Turner put his finger on the two at the end, the girl and a tall, thin man. "We've seen those two before," he said and straightened up.

They certainly had. That couple was in the photo in Dan Grady's wallet. The only thing missing was the toddler. *A toddler who would be about the same age as Emily Martin.* Harvey pulled out the pin and lifted the photo to the light. He couldn't tell who the other two were. Chances were that by now, those two boys had grown into men with paunches and less hair. He flipped the picture over and hit pay-dirt.

Four names stretched across the back, the lettering faded but legible. *Lily, Bobby-O, Ray and Phil.* "Ray and Phil," he said, "are the two that inherited this place. Lily is buried in the graveyard, the last person to be interred there."

"How do you know that?" Turner asked.

Harvey grinned, at last something that Turner didn't know. "I took Lem's History and Ghost Walking Tour when I first started working here," he said. "You should try it."

He flicked the photo with his forefinger. "The fellow beside Lily, I'm thinking he's our victim, Dan Grady. Looks different for sure but, given we found that photo in his wallet, it's him. That would explain the connection between Phil and him. There was a lot of money went missing when Phil went to jail. Want to bet Grady took off with it?"

Turner shook his head. Harvey wasn't surprised. Turner rarely bet and never when the odds were against him.

Harvey turned back to the maps and tide charts. He tapped on one. "I saw this place on the map. That's Horseshoe Bay. If we head out across the front lawn," he said, pointing toward the ocean, "we'd be looking at it." He leaned closer and peered at the photographs. A dark line ran across the joined photos, intersecting some caves, underlining others and passing over the top of at least one. Harvey read the scrawled label. "High tide line."

Why had Phil been interested in these caves? None of them were safe. He tapped on the cave with the high tide line running over the top. A big red circle marked it and numbers marched down the side. He compared them to the tide charts. "Looks like next high tide is about 12:59 a.m." He glanced at his watch. "That's about now."

If Emily and Marta were stashed in the cave, was their kidnapper with them? What did he plan to do and when?

Harvey's phone rang. "Conrad here."

"It's Devon. We found a track off the road over the dunes. There's a small boat pulled up into the sea grass. It's wet. Been used lately." He heard the breath she drew in before continuing. "And Harvey, Marta's cane is in the bottom of the boat."

Damn, sometimes he hated when his instincts were right.

CHAPTER 18

Emily lay curled on the ledge. Time passed. *Enough already.* She took her hands down from her head. She kept her eyes closed and envisioned a wide open space, sunshine and room to run. Her fear decreased to a simmer.

Phil had said he might just leave her there to die. *Damn, I don't want to starve.* Her stomach gurgled as if in agreement. She'd read somewhere that if you had water, you could last up to two months. Maybe there was fresh water dripping off the rocks. She gave herself a mental slap on the head. Someone would miss her and look for her before she died of starvation. If she had not been so fuzzy-headed from the drugs Phil gave her, she'd have thought of that earlier. No, he couldn't risk just leaving her there. He had a plan he hadn't mentioned.

Either way, lying here doing nothing does not help. At least take inventory.

She was on a ledge above the water. She extended one leg until her toes hit water. The level wasn't any higher than before. *The tide has stopped rising. And I am not dead.* She raised her arm and before it was fully extended, her hand connected with rock. *This ceiling has been here, solidly holding up the earth, for eons of time. It won't collapse on me.* For the moment, the space she was in did not threaten her life. So much for the geography of her predicament.

Now to the human factor. Phil probably wouldn't take her out of there. And Daddy wasn't going to come and find her this time. *If I lie here and do nothing, I can die. If I move, I might live. Living is good. There are people out there who could be friends.*

There's Harvey, the cop. Harvey? When did I start thinking about him with his first name? Harvey, with his practical manner and his solid, warm body would look for her, and he'd find her. Her situation seemed suddenly a bit better.

She breathed in. *There is air. I won't smother.* She rolled onto her knees and felt around with her hands. One hand plunged in the water, and she lost her balance, rolled and hit the cold, gasping, as she sank under the surface. The shock stopped her breath for a heartbeat. She kicked and came up sputtering and clawing at the ledge. Fright once again had her by the neck. *Wow, that took care of the brain-fog.*

She struggled, clinging to the ledge. *I'm freezing cold, up to my neck in sea water, in the dark, and with no way out. I need to fight.* She kicked again, rose enough to get her forearms onto the ledge. A few more kicks and her stomach cleared the water and pressed painfully against the rock edge. She reached with one hand, seeking leverage. Her fingers closed around a rocky outcropping and, between pulling and crawling, she made it back onto the ledge.

Shivering, she pushed up on all fours and hit her head. *Ouch. Need to remember the low overhead.* A warm trickle feathered down her right temple. Damn, she'd cut her head again. Her soaked jacket dragged at her. She took it off and set it aside. Soaking wet it didn't offer any heat. She removed her sneakers and dumped out water. Taking off her socks, she squeezed out as much water as she could, shook them and put them back. They might be wet, but she needed her feet protected.

More or less sorted out, she edged forward in a commando crawl and smacked the crown of her head. *A wall. This isn't working. Slow down and get a plan.*

Kneeling on the rock, she hugged herself. *You are not five years old anymore. You have skills. You can get out of here.* She could hear water slapping against rock and smell the chill rising from its surface. Her eyes saw only black. She licked her lips and tasted the salt. Shivering against the cold, and the heavy wetness the water had left in her clothing, she pushed her brain to come up with an idea. *I have all the senses but sight. So I need to use the senses I have.*

How high is the opening from the cave to the ocean? Could she swim underwater and get out? Hell, who was she kidding, she didn't swim underwater. If Phil didn't return, maybe she could swim out when the tide went down. But what waited outside? A safe shore? She had no idea.

It was, however, tempting to wait and see if he came. Maybe she could find a loose rock and bash him when he arrived. *But if I fail?*

He might kill me or tie me up so I couldn't move or swim. No. I need to act now. She gulped, tears and crazy laughter vied for precedence. *Action is the only option.*

But what action? *Think, girl, think.* She lay on her side and curled her knees to her body and hugged them, trying to get some warmth. *Duh. Of course, maybe there is an airshaft. Lem talked about airshafts.* And he said the only cave big enough to accommodate things or people had an airshaft. It had to be this one. She had to find it. She put both hands on her skull and pressed. The headache from banging her head was not helping. *Find a stick to use like blind people do.* No sticks around her. *Use your hands.* She extended her reach and let her hands do her looking. A picture of a narrow, low-ceilinged cavern formed in her head. *The only open space is away from the water. Time to move. Just make it straight back.*

She checked the location of the water, and commando crawled again, as straight back as she could figure. She adjusted as she sensed the cavern widening. Several maneuvers later, her fingers connected with fabric. She froze for a nanosecond and jerked her hand away. What the heck? She lowered her hand once more, letting it rest on the fabric. She pressed harder. The surface gave slightly under her touch. She squeezed gently. Flesh? A low moan startled her and she jerked, hitting her head. *A live body.* She was not alone. Who was in the cave with her?

"Hello?" The whispered word flattened in the small space. She tried again. "Hello. Are you okay?" The flat sound was too weird. Another moan rolled through the cave. The person must be unconscious. She moved closer and started patting. *So damn dark. Dark enough for bats or rats. No, no, no, don't go there.*

She continued her exploration. A small face and long hair. A woman. She was wearing an apron. Who the heck wore an apron anymore? Emily ran her hands down each leg and, at the end of the second one, came to a laced boot with a metal cradle. She sat back on her haunches, careful this time not to bang her head. The person with her was Marta from the grocery store. Why on earth had Phil put her in here? And what had he done to her? How badly was she hurt?

This complicated things. Not only did she have to get herself out of there, she had to help this woman. Emily sat with her eyes closed.

No point in opening them in the absolute darkness.

She could lie beside the woman and offer added body heat. A vision of two skeletons, side by side, flashed in her head. Besides, she was soaked and shivering. How much heat did she have to offer? However, if she failed to find a shaft, she could come back and stay with Marta then.

She buried her face in her hands and tears clumped in her throat. *Why did I come here? Why did I ever feel the need to know my roots? I'm cold, wet and could die in this dark, damp hole. How has it come to this?*

She huffed out air, brushed her fingers firmly over her cheeks and squared her shoulders. *Stop the pity party—now.* A puff of air caressed her face. Air? Moving air? She licked a finger and held it up. *That's how they determine wind direction in the movies.* The faint movement of air brushed her finger, coming from further back in the cave. Hope washed over her as cool and restoring as the tiny blast of air. If she could find where it was coming in, she might find a way out.

She put two fingers under the woman's chin. Her pulse was strong and steady. So maybe, she was just out from drugs. Time to leave her for now. The woman coughed and stirred. She couldn't be any more comfortable than Emily. *What to do, what to do?* She felt for the woman's forehead. It was cool and damp. That was good, wasn't it? *Oh my, I am having a conversation with myself.*

Don't waste time sitting here. Get moving. Emily edged past the prone figure and crawled toward the back of the cave, cringing as rocks battered her palms and knees. Suddenly she felt air on the back of her head. That meant it was coming from above. She sat back cautiously and put her hand straight up. Her fingers met only air. Finding the wall, she edged up until she was standing. Her knees and hands almost sighed in relief. Another hand upwards and still only empty space.

Laughter bubbled out of her, driven by relief and infused with tears. She'd found the airshaft.

. . . . .

Harvey shut off the phone and tapped it against his hand. "Whoever it is, they have Marta too." He explained about the boat.

"And it tells us the kidnapper isn't in the cave right now."

The rookie turned from the pictures. "Do you think he plans to go back?"

"That is yet to be determined. Depends on what he wants with them." Harvey screwed up his mouth. "If Grady was one of the thieves back in the day, maybe he still had some of the money. Millions went missing." He looked at Turner. "What do you think?"

"If Martin is connected to Grady, maybe this fellow thinks she has the money, or knows where it is."

"Possible. But Marta? I don't get the connection, unless she saw him snatch Emily and became unwanted collateral." Harvey pocketed the phone. "Okay—you two keep searching. Turner, you're with me." He pulled a map of the cliff and caves off of the wall. "Let's go check on this boat."

He phoned the two officers still at the store. "Lock it up tight, call out the Crime Scene Unit and you two go man the bridge. No one on the island except our people, and no one off." He clicked off the phone and pointed to the road behind the dunes.

Turner made the corner and slowed. Harvey saw the track Devon had explained to him and they turned toward where the women had found the boat. Turner pulled up beside Gwen's car. Not only were Devon, Kelsey and Gwen there, Hart and Dave Lamont were with them. As Harvey approached, Devon waved her cell phone at him.

"I called Lem about the caves. He says only one of the caves in Horseshoe Bay is big enough to hide anything or anybody." She pursed her lips. "And that one has its entrance underwater at high tide which is about now."

Harvey nodded. "Confirms what we found." He looked at the boat, an aluminum rowboat with an outboard motor. The rising moon glinted off Marta's cane.

The group looked at him. If he didn't come up with a plan, no doubt one of them would. And it might not be the safest plan around.

"Do something," Dave demanded, stepping closer to Harvey. "Marta has heart issues, she's not strong. We need to get her out of there."

How did he know that? And what was it to him? Harvey sighed.

"Oh," Devon said. "Lem said a shaft comes out somewhere in the field the other side of the Oickle place." She frowned. "But they covered it with a wooden top and dirt years ago. Probably solidly buried by now. Don't know how we'll find it."

Damn woman. She could have led with that bit of information. He looked at the boat. He knew nothing about boat motors or rowing. "Who can drive that boat?" he asked.

Hart raised a hand. "I was junior, dory racing champion three years running," he said with a grin. "And I can work the motor."

Well, that was one option. Harvey turned and looked at Turner. "How about you?"

Turner shrugged. "Had a rowboat on the dug-out back home," he said. "I can row and swim."

"Good deal," Harvey said, coming to an abrupt decision. "You and Hart launch that thing and go find the mouth of the cave. Here are the pictures and maps. You may not get in right now, but you'll be there if we need you." He paused. "And in case our man comes back. Stay in contact."

Devon poked Hart on the shoulder. "No heroics, eh?"

The kid crossed his heart and raised a hand. "Promise."

"That's what you said the last time," she muttered and glared at him.

What was that about? Harvey looked from one to the other. He'd check it out later. Right now they needed to get moving.

"You four are with me. We're off to the field. If you have flashlights, or a shovel, this would be the time to show them. Devon, get me Lem on the phone. I need to figure out a search grid." He pulled out his own phone and rang the rookie. "Lock up tight with chains and some of our locks. Don't want anyone to get in and destroy evidence do we? We'll be there soon. We have a search to conduct. And check around for a shovel."

He rang off and pointed at Devon. "You can drive with me. We need to talk."

. . . . .

Phil eased around the curve, heading toward the house from the south. He'd checked on the aspects the boss had requested and called them in. The van's lights cut a swath in the darkness. He glanced ahead. Lights on in the house? He hadn't left them on. He stomped on the brake and backed around the corner. Finding an overgrown trail, he eased the van in and locked it up. Keeping to the tree line, and the dark shade in the ditch, he walked quickly toward the house. Diagonally across from it, he sought deeper shelter. Two cars. Police cars. His face twitched. The cops were in his house.

The perfectly organized maps and charts would be his undoing. Even a dumb cop could figure out what he was up to. He clenched his fists and ground his teeth. *Bloody, damn cops.* He turned and paced in the tiny space between two trees. He ran his hand over his hair, slammed one fist into the other palm and then pounded it against a tree.

The pain registered and he stopped, leaned forward and propped his hands on his knees. Getting back into the cave before they figured things out wasn't an option. The tide was still too high, the moonlight too bright. And he couldn't swim even if he did get to the mouth of the cave undetected.

He returned to watching the house. The only thing he could do was run. *Running is for wimps.* Too bad. Not running could put him back in jail. And that wasn't going to happen. Not unless he'd killed that precious little Suzie-Q first. Marta could live. Serve her right to have the rest of them dead. All he could do would be to find a way to hide out, regroup and try again. He ignored the mocking voice in his head that chanted—*fat chance, sucker.* He'd find a way.

First step, find a vehicle. He could do that. He had both sets of keys. Marta had a car. Emily had a truck. He started walking, staying about two feet inside the tree line. From there he could catch glimpses of the road, and would have time to hide if any vehicles came along. Once he was mobile, he'd head for the furthest island, the one at the end of the road. The big cottages on that third island sat on secluded sites and were only used occasionally. There would be boats if he needed to get off the islands. Yes. That worked. He could do that.

Nah, nah, you think you can but you can't. And what about the money. If you don't find it....

Oh, shut up. Phil banished the doubting voice in his head and pressed on. He no longer cared if his high-and-mighty cousin got his precious millions back. It was dirty money anyway. And he sure as hell wouldn't get any of it.

By the time Phil reached where the south loop of the road joined the main one, sweat poured down his face, bugs tasted his blood and a branch or two had smacked him. He waited and listened. No car motors. After a quick look in both directions, he darted across the road and into the far trees. They would only protect him for so long. Then he'd need to go around the back of the old cemetery and manse and past the back of that gift store that used to be the church. After that, it wasn't far to the back of Marta's garage.

Before starting, Phil ran his path in his head. *Doable.* He dodged through the trees and headed for the back of the graveyard. He'd be out of there and safely on his way in no time.

. . . . .

Emily closed her eyes in the darkness, and crossed her hands on her chest. *Breathe in, breathe out. Steady now. Don't hyperventilate.* She bowed her head and one quick thank you flowed into the dark. *Now, get going.*

She squatted and checked the floor. There seemed be three carved and smooth steps. People had been here in the past. She stood, keeping one hand on the wall and the other over her head. When she reached the third step, she helicoptered her hands above her and mapped the size of the space. Not large but not tiny. She extended her hands to the walls, and measuring the width, breathed a sigh of relief. So far, the shaft felt wide enough to allow her access.

Moments later she had her fingers wedged in the crack above her. She reached higher with the other hand and found a rocky outcropping. *I need footholds.* She pulled herself up, scrambling with her feet until she found toeholds to support her. Her arches cramped. Her fingers screamed for relief. *Are you really going up there?* She pushed and pulled until she was higher in the shaft. Her heart pounded and her breath came is short puffs. *Get a grip. You can panic when you get out of here.*

Once more she searched with her hands, found purchase and pulled up, ignoring the searing heat in her biceps. One foot found a protruding rock. The other she extended to the far side of the shaft and wedged it in what felt like a crack. Braced there, her muscles could ease and the cramps in her feet relax. One clawing move after another, she edged up the shaft. Air puffed against the side of her face. She closed her eyes and tipped her head back, reaching with her senses to find the source.

It's not coming straight down? Does the shaft bend?

No-no. I can't do a corner. I'll be stuck.
 Weight crushed her mind and clenched her lungs. She gasped. *Stop it. There is air. If all else fails, you can go down again.*
 The thought of going down, of failing to evade Phil and to get help for Marta, jumpstarted her breathing. *I can do this.* She reached again, sweeping one hand back and forth, and found the air source. The channel was small, barely wide enough for her hand. *Please, please. This can't be the end.*
 Tears rolled down her face, the salt stinging a cut on her cheek. She swept the hand again and the openness directly above her registered. *Two shafts. One has air. One goes up.*
 Emily drew in several breaths of fresh air and resumed her climb. Inch by hard-won inch she moved through the narrow shaft in the cocoon of darkness. *How long have I been climbing?* She paused, and rested her muscles. One after the other, she brought her hands to her mouth and checked her fingers. Dirt and blood lingered on her tongue. *I need to go on. Right hand gripping. Left hand clinging by the fingers. Right foot solid against an outcropping. Ready, go.*
 Emily pushed with her right leg, pulled with her hands and propelled herself upward in one huge heaving motion. Thump. Her ears rang and even in the dark she saw stars. *Oh, that hurts.* She pressed against the wall and clung tightly, fighting her body's urge to go limp.
 That wasn't rock. She put up one hand. *Wood. A cover?* Laughter and tears mingled. Sobs and hiccups bounced in the narrow space. *I've reached the top.*

. . . . .

 Harvey pulled into the yard at Enos Oickle's house and turned the car lights on the south field. Thick, overgrown grass covered the landscape. Here and there a single bush flourished. Piles of rocks looked abandoned by some would-be farmer trying to clear the field for planting. How on earth would they find the top of the shaft? He left the lights on and got out of the car. And if they did, would anyone be able to get down it?
 He flicked on his flashlight and turned to meet the second car. "How many flashlights?"
 Gwen held up one and Dave Lamont another. Both the rookie

and his partner had flashlights. The rookie grinned and held up a shovel and two long crowbars. Good thinking. Poking the earth might find them the wooden cover. They were as ready as they could be.

Harvey looked at the assortment of searchers. "Lem said the shaft came out somewhere between the cave and the house and not too far inland from the edge of the cliff. At least as far as he can remember from what the oldtimers said. We'll make a line running back from the cliff-edge and, starting by the house, work our way south." He pulled out his phone and dialed.

"Turner, what's your progress?"

"Just off the cave opening. No flat shoreline anywhere in the horseshoe. We can just see the top arch of what we think is our target. No clear air yet."

"Shine your light on the opening and then raise the beam upwards to the clifftop to give us a point of reference."

"Roger." The light beam appeared and they took their positions.

"And tell Hart to stay in the damn boat - no heroics." Devon had filled him in on Hart's part in capturing a killer six years back. He did not want the kid playing hero any more than she had.

He hung up. The others were already at the edge of the field. He joined them and, at arms-length spacing, they started their search. Stomping, stabbing the ground with an iron bar, he moved forward. How exactly they'd find the right spot he had no idea. All they could do was try.

. . . . .

Emily braced both feet on one side of the shaft and her back against the rock face behind her. At the top of the shaft the air was warmer, almost muggy. Although eager to get out, she forced herself to rest. Finally, she bent her head and, like Atlas holding up the world, got her shoulders against the wood. She pushed, but it did not move. Eyes closed, she regulated her breathing, gathering strength for a second try.

Shifting carefully, she edged the top of her back against the planks. With arms spread to brace on the sides of the shaft, she pushed, using all the energy she could summon. Nothing happened. She drew in another deep breath and pushed again, holding the force as long as her shaking legs allowed. Nothing. Darkness tightened around her. She was trapped from above.

In sheer frustration, she screamed, and the sound bounced against the rock. Tears welled once again in her eyes. *There has to be a way.* She pushed again. *It moved. I felt it. Just a little, but it moved.* She pushed again, and crumbs of soil rained down on her. *It's going to work. It has to work.*

She adjusted her position and pushed again. Her feet slipped and she fell, banging and scraping against the shaft walls, until she managed a precarious purchase on protruding rock. Sobbing, ignoring the blood trickling from many scrapes, she edged up to the top again. Her whole body screamed against the indignity of the bumps and cuts. She pushed but had only minimal gain. Again, dirt fell on her. *Try another tactic.*

She reached up, found the perimeter of the wood, and shoved her fingers into the dirt. She pushed until her fingers refused to go further. She curled two fingers, pulling dirt out of the crack. Pain sliced her fingernails and knuckles. How much dirt was up there? Years' worth? It would take her forever. She hung her head and let the sobs wrack her chest and the tears bathe her face.

Moments later, she dug at the dirt again and then, placing her back against the cover, pushed as hard as she could. *I am not giving up.* The tiny gain was not enough to free her. She screamed, gritted her teeth and banged her bleeding hands against the wood. "Damn it. Move. Let. Me. Out." Her words echoed in the shaft. Her own voice faded to nothing.

"Emily, Emily. Can you hear me?"

Emily tilted her head. It sounded as if the voices were below her. But they couldn't have gotten into the cave. The calls came again. *The secondary shaft. The sounds are coming in there. But they know where I am.* Laughter jerked in and out in a rhythm more suited to sobbing.

She banged on the cover and hollered again. "Here, I'm here."

"Keep calling." The voice sounded closer. Thudding joined the voice. "Can you hear us stomping our feet?"

"Yes," Her dry throat clogged.

"Hot or cold?"

I remember the hot and cold game.

"Hot. Keep coming." And then the thuds were right over her

head and dirt dislodged by the stomping fell on her.

"Hot. Right there." She slumped and gave over to tears. *Hold on. I need to hold on. They'll get me out.*

"We have her." *Sounded like Devon.* Running footsteps shuddered against the ground.

A scraping thump and rasp joined the voices. *It sounds like a shovel.* More dirt fell on her, and she kept her face down, letting it fall against her head and shoulders. *Never thought I'd like a dirt shower.*

The dirt stopped, the wood groaned and the cover disappeared. Night air whooshed in around her. She looked up. Stars. Moonlight. And three faces peering down at her. Devon, Kelsey and Gwen.

"You know," Kelsey said, her voice thick with tears. "If you didn't want to join the club you only had to say so. This is a bit extreme."

Emily laughed through her tears, straightened her legs and taking two of the hands extended toward her, forced her shoulders into the open. Strong fingers gripped her under the arms and pulled. Emily surged into the open and knelt on the grass. Looked up. Not only the three women, but also Harvey and Dave stood there. She folded forward and collapsed on the ground with tears running down her face. Battered, bruised and bleeding, but safe. *I made it.*

"There's water in the cruiser," Harvey said, and Devon took off running.

"Phil," Emily managed to say. "He said he'd be back." She coughed, her throat scratchy. "Kill us."

"Marta, where is Marta?" One hand on her shoulder, Dave was almost shaking her.

Harvey pulled him away. "Hang on there, buddy. We'll get the answers."

Devon returned and Gwen lifted Emily to a seated position. She sipped the water.

Kelsey had removed her jacket and now slipped it over Emily's shoulders.

Emily hugged it close. Her head throbbed. "Marta is down there—unconscious but above the water line. Pulse steady." Emily's aching body reminded her of the arduous climb. No way could Marta come up the shaft, even with help. How would they get her out? Would they have to wait for the tide?

Gwen pocketed her phone. "Jackson and Lem are on the way with the ambulance."

"Can you get down there?" Emily asked. "There's climbing gear, ropes, in the storage unit of my trailer."

"Good to know." Harvey, down on one knee beside her, checked her pulse.

Warm fingers. Rough skin.

The ambulance siren sounded from the road, one long blast. Emily closed her eyes and drifted. When she opened them again, Lem and Jackson had joined the group.

Jackson held up his hand. "Focus on my fingers, Emily. How many?"

Emily tried. All she saw was a blur. She took a guess. "Two."

"Close but not quite." Jackson turned her head to the side. "That's quite a blow she's got. Lot of blood." He muttered as he examined her. "I'd say she's concussed. We'll take her in."

"There's a second ambulance coming from the hospital for Marta." Lem's voice. Rustling went on around her without further conversation.

A neck brace appeared around her neck. Movement beside her drew her attention. She turned her head. The stretcher.

"Okay then, hang on, Emily."

Hang on to what?

Harvey aligned her body and crossed her arms on her chest. Moving to her head, he slid his hands, warm, solid and secure, under her shoulders. Someone else's strong fingers folded around her legs and other arms tucked under her lower back.

"On a count of three." Jackson's voice. And then she was floating, lifted up and over and coming to rest on the stretcher. They strapped her in and put something in her arm.

An IV. It would be an IV.

Emily's mind drifted. Her aches and pains faded. Blankets covered her and tucked around her. She closed her eyes and gave control over to the rescuers. They'd saved her. They'd save Marta. All sound disappeared.

. . . . .

Phil was behind the graveyard when he heard the ambulance

siren. One long blast. *They couldn't have found them. They're in the cave.* What happened? He chuckled. Maybe one of the officers had fallen off the cliff or something. He waited until the ambulance passed, moving fast. No worries, he'd get out of there before they found him. He moved silently through the shrubbery until he was behind the garage. He waited again. Heard no sounds. Saw no lights. Edging along the dark, south side, he found the man-door and gained access to the garage.

Outside, the building was old with wooden clapboard siding. Inside, he felt his way to the car and opened the driver's door. He needed light to see how the big garage door opened. The car's overhead lamp shone faint light around him. Phil blinked. The walls were drywalled and, up in the corner, a heater hung from the finished ceiling. He extended his exploration. Bonus. Someone had installed an overhead, automatic door opener.

He slid into the car, pressed the door button and heard the motor whir overhead. About to start the engine, he paused. The ambulance was once again using its siren. And it was coming this way. He waited until it passed and, letting them get a head start, pulled onto the road behind them. Who did they have in the vehicle?

At the bridge, the ambulance slowed and stopped. A uniformed officer stepped up to the window as the driver lowered it. On the night air, their voice carried easily to where Phil waited.

"Did you find them?"

"Yes. Emily Martin climbed up the airshaft. She's in bad shape but not critical. There'll be one of the ambulance rigs from town along in a bit to get the storekeeper. She's still in the cave."

The uniformed officer knocked on the side of the van. "Good job."

Phil muttered obscenities. That damn girl was too smart for her own good. A shaft. How had he missed that? And who'd think it would be big enough to allow her to climb up it? He put the car in gear and, without looking toward the officers, drove at a modest speed toward the bridge to the second island. *She can't get away. She has to die. I can't stop now. I need a new plan. I have to kill her. It's my duty to Becky.*

There hadn't seemed to be any cops following the ambulance. If he could get to the hospital in good time, he might be able to use that syringe in his pocket. No meds left in it, but all he needed to kill her was a good-sized air bubble or two pumped into her artery. He chuckled, once again focused on his task. All was not lost.

Phil starting humming. *Farewell to Nova Scotia* floated through the car. Farewell well indeed. He'd send her to a place she could never come back from.

CHAPTER 19

Harvey went to the top of the shaft and directed the flashlight beam into the opening. Good heavens. How had she managed to get through that space? He eyed the width. No way was he getting down there. Dave came up beside him.

"Lenya is going for the climbing gear," he said, "and blankets. The ropes will let us get things down the shaft."

"Probably a thermos of tea as well," Harvey muttered as he sized up the man. *Nope. Lamont is not getting down there either.* Who did that leave? Gwen's short height and well-rounded body wouldn't be ideal. Kelsey was pregnant. He looked at Devon. *It'll have to be her.*

He dialed Turner. "Anything happening on the water?"

"No." Turner hesitated. "Not on the water."

"What does that mean?"

"Um, Hart has removed his cap, his shoes and his jacket and trousers."

"What?" Harvey's shout brought everyone running to his side. "You tell him to get his clothes back on and stay put."

"Tried that. He's a bit stubborn."

Harvey dropped the flashlight and plunked himself on the forehead with his free hand. *Save me from wannabe heroes.*

Devon dropped to one knee beside him. "Hart?"

Harvey nodded to her and spoke to Turner. "What does he think he is up to?"

"Going to swim underwater and get into the cave. Says he has the first aid needed to take care of Marta. Says you can lower equipment to him. He'll find the opening for the shaft as soon as he has assessed her."

Harvey shook his head. "Put that dumbbell on the phone." A splash followed his words.

"Too late," Turner said.

"Get as close to the cave as you can," Harvey directed. "And be ready to haul his sorry ass into the boat if he has to come back." He smacked his thumb against the off button.

"What is it with you people?"

No one answered his rhetorical question.

. . . . .

Phil's slow drive across the bridge to the second island ended, and he pushed the little car as fast as he dared on the narrow, winding road. The third bridge, narrower than the other two, loomed ahead. He pulled a skidding turn and rattled across the bridge on the one-way lane. Once on the third island, he slowed and watched for properties. He knew the east side of the island. They had established a spot to unload incoming cargo. But he didn't want that side.

He pictured the map in his head and headed for the northwest side. That location would be farther from the first two islands and closer to the mainland. The few properties there had locked gates, not that locks were an issue for him. But locked gates might indicate vacant properties. Good thing it was near the end of August. Most folks had headed home to get their kiddies ready for the school year.

He finished the full circuit of the island before stopping in front of a property whose location fitted his needs. He pulled the car to the far side of the road and set out on foot. For now he simply hopped over the two bars locking out vehicles. He checked the house for action and found none. But it wasn't the house he was interested in. His primary goal was the large boathouse nestled between a boat launch and a fancy dock.

Thin shafts of daylight spiked up from the horizon. The locks on the boathouse proved challenging, but he opened them in the end. Inside he found a locked room that was easier to access. A board with keys gave him what he needed for both the 240 BowRider and the locks on the water-doors. What he knew about boats would fill a shot glass, but the sleek unit, bobbing beside the inside dock, looked like it was built for speed.

Jogging, he returned to the car, picked the lock on the front gate, and after pulling the car in on the driveway, put the bars and locks back in place. Back in the car, he followed the drive past the house and around to the boat launch. His heart pounded and hot blood surged through him. The previous plan forgotten, he hummed as he completed the current step in his new plan to kill Emily Martin.

He lined the car up on the concrete launch apron and, placing a large rock on the accelerator, put it in gear and slammed the door shut. The little red car roared forward, skimmed a few feet and sank nose-down where deeper water edged the bottom of the ramp.

Yee haw, that was great! He raised his hands in a boxer's winning stance and, after a few fancy steps, headed for the boathouse. Now to go after Emily Martin aka Suzie-Q. The only thing better than sinking the car would be injecting air bubbles into her or her IV and watching her die of a heart attack or stroke. Better if it was a heart attack. Recovery from a stroke happened more often than from a heart attack. Or at least he thought so. Either way, she'd get her comeuppance.

. . . . .

Harvey stood by as Devon and the rookie lowered a blanket roll down the shaft. They'd put a cell phone, a flashlight and water inside the roll. They lowered, paused, pulled back and, giving it a shake, lowered it some more. How long was this going to take? Not knowing if Hart had made it through, or if Marta was still alive, didn't help his mood.

The phone in his hand rang. He checked the caller ID. "Hart?" At an affirmative answer he went on. "What the hell do you think you're doing? We don't need another person to rescue."

Hart laughed. "No worries. I'm fine." His tone sobered. "Marta is alive but cold. She was shivering when I got here. Her pulse is erratic and her breathing shallow. I'm worried about hypothermia and shock. I've got the blanket around her but could use a few more. These rocks are too cold for her to be lying on them."

"Right. They'll be down in a few minutes." Harvey had to admit that the kid knew what he was doing. He glanced over to where the rope had been pulled back up the shaft. "More blankets and the first aid kit," he directed.

Lenya stepped up with another roll of blankets. "Three," she said, patting the blankets, "and a bottle of orange juice and some hard candies as well as a first aid kit." The second bundle disappeared down the hole.

Harvey waited, keeping the line open between him and Hart. Minutes ticked by and he heard Hart's voice. He seemed to be soothing Marta. Good kid, even if he was a bit brash. Hart came back on the line. "I found a stuffed frog down here. I've used it under her head. It's not damp or moldy so it has not been here for a long time."

A frog? There had been a stuffed frog in the window at Emily's trailer. He thought back. Why frogs? What was with the live ones and the stuffed one?

Hart came back on the line. "Thanks. Got some water and juice into her and have her well wrapped. She does not seem to have any cuts or bruises. From what she said, he must have drugged her. But she's alert now. Did you catch the guy?"

"Not yet."

"Marta says he promised to kill Emily Martin, come hell or high water. We've had the high water, but don't know about hell. Not telling you your job, but maybe it's wise to have a guard on her until the fellow is caught?"

"Noted. How much longer before you can get the boat in there and get her out?"

"Maybe an hour or ninety minutes. Then, as long as we put her flat in the boat, I can swim behind and push the boat out. Turner will have to figure out how to get it in here."

"I'll let him know. Have to go. I have another call coming in." And Harvey rang off.

"Conrad here."

"Jane at dispatch here. We just had a call. The alarms have gone off at a house on the third island. Owner called it in. Said the boathouse alarm was triggered. It's silent at that end so whoever did it might not know. Thought it might be related to your situation."

Harvey cursed under his breath and turned his back to a gust of off-shore wind.

"Sorry, sir, I didn't catch that."

"Not relevant. Thanks for letting me know. Can you get a member over to the hospital to guard Emily Martin?"

"I'll see what I can do, sir. But your situation has a lot of people already assigned. Will you send a car over to the other island? And I don't know how soon I can get someone over to the hospital."

"Call the hospital then. Tell them to keep an eye on her in the meantime. No visitors until I get there. I'll send someone to check on the boathouse."

"Right, sir. Will do." And Jane ended the call.

Harvey signaled for the rookie and his partner to join him and filled them in. "I'm guessing it was our friend, Phil, who got into the boathouse." He turned to the rookie. Seemed that in spite of his newness on the coast, he'd had experience at his previous posting. "Can you handle this? You need to stay here in contact with Hart. When they get Marta in the boat, you all need to head for the dunes. Direct the ambulance over there."

"Yes sir, I can do that."

"I'll do what I can to help," Dave said. "I may be retired but my brain still works."

"You." Harvey pointed at the other officer. "Get over to the third island. Get the location from dispatch and check the boathouse. Find out what type of boats should be there and put out a bulletin on whatever one is missing."

"Are we sure one is missing?"

"Trust me, one is. If not, I'll eat my socks." Harvey took one more look around, nodded to Devon and, patting Lenya on the shoulder, headed for his cruiser. This wasn't over yet.

Chapter 20

Jolted from a warm dark place, Emily cringed against the clatter, the motion and the lights appearing overhead. The brightness soaked through the protection of her eyelids and she scrunched her face. Pain followed. She stopped scrunching and attempted to bring up her arm to protect her eyes. It moved a few inches and caught on something. She tugged.

"Hang on, miss," a deep, authoritative voice said. "We have your arms secured for safety."

Enough of all this nonsense. I need to get it together.

She clenched her gut and sucked enough air to make her voice work. "What are you doing to me?" It wasn't much more than a croak, but it was coherent.

"She's awake," said a voice, a female this time. The sensation of someone close to her face washed over her and came with a question. "Can you open your eyes?"

"Too bloody bright," she said.

The woman gave a short laugh. "I think she's going to be okay. No worries, dear, just give us a minute." And she was as good as her word.

Emily's conveyance clattered on, rocking her gently and triggering waves of dizziness. But finally she ended up in a dimmer spot. The shade bathed her eyelids, and she risked opening her eyes. Both worked. Someone must have unstuck them. Tile ceiling, metal runners and curtains on either side.

"Why am I in a hospital?" she muttered, but they heard her. She closed her eyes. Brief images flashed across her consciousness but she couldn't make them stop long enough to figure them out.

"You had a nasty blow to the head," the woman said. "When you were climbing out of the shaft." She bustled, and moments later Emily felt herself slung from what she now surmised was a gurney onto a hard bed. And then the woman was back, tucking a sheet under Emily's chin and clanking up the side rails. "Can you tell us your name?"

Name? They want my name? Don't they have it? Why are they asking? Do they think it's not real? Suzie Wilson? No, that was the old one. Come on, think.

"I think the concussion is worse than we thought. She doesn't seem to know her name."

Relief flashed through her. They just wanted to make sure her brain was working. "Sorry," she said. "Water."

They brought a sponge on a stick and wiped her mouth and let her have a sip of cool water.

"Thanks," she said. "Much better. Emily Martin," she added. "My name is Emily Martin." The lie slipped easily off her tongue. Years of practice saw to that. Plus, she'd closed her eyes. They would not see her lie. They would hear what they expected to hear.

"Do you know what day it is?"

"Should be Wednesday night, I think. How long was I out?"

"Not that long. You were okay at first, but took a bad turn in the ambulance."

"Then it might be Thursday morning by now." She risked opening her eyes. Saw spotted dogs on a field of pink. Uniform top. A nurse.

"And do you know where you are?"

"I'd say this is a hospital. I have no idea where it is."

The woman patted her shoulder. "Good enough. You'll make it. The doctor will be along momentarily." And the woman swished out, flipping the curtain closed behind her.

Emily dozed, knowing she was safe. Gradually, the images from the cave and the airshaft coalesced and she remembered. She'd climbed up. But she had fallen and banged her body up quite a bit. That included her head apparently. Her left arm itched. She lifted it to scratch it, but couldn't. It was encased in white bandage from hand to just above the elbow. She dozed again.

Marta! Phil!

The memory pushed her heart into overdrive. The machine at the head of the bed beeped like a crazed chicken. The nurse appeared at the side of the bed. She pushed a button and the beeping stopped.

"What happened? You're reacting as if you were frightened?"

"He's going to kill her." Emily paused and licked her lips. "I had to leave her in the cave." She struggled to sit up. The nurse gently pushed her back.

"Don't worry. Your ambulance driver said the police were on the scene and that the ambulance dispatched from here would be bringing us another patient soon. They'll take care of her."

Emily's neck muscles stopped straining, and she let her head fall back on the pillow. Relief washed through her. She closed her eyes. "Thanks. Will you let me know when they bring her in?"

"Sure will." The nurse adjusted a tube, smoothed the pillow and left.

. . . . .

Phil pointed the boat toward the mainland, working to organize the geography in his head. He'd spent enough time checking everything out for bringing in the drugs. He should be able to maximize his position.

The sun, rising over the horizon, gave him his east point. If he headed north and slightly west, he should find the mouth of the inlet that ran into the LaHave River. He'd have to bet on them taking her to Bridgewater. The river ended outside the town, so at that point, he'd have to ditch the boat and find a vehicle. He loved all the trees in this province. They provided lots of places to hide out. It shouldn't be too hard to find a car. An old one would be best—easier to hot-wire. Some of those new ones were impossible.

The wind blew in his face and the boat twanged as it flew from wave to wave. Not a bad way to travel. He'd have to try it again when he had more time to enjoy it. Right now the speed thrummed through the soles of his feet and vibrated up his legs. *Magnificent.* He found the inlet and slowed as he headed up river. He didn't want to attract attention. And he sure didn't want to hit a hidden log.

He checked his watch. Hadn't taken him that long. When the river narrowed, he found a secluded spot on the left riverbank and pulled the BowRider to shore. He should sink it, but couldn't bring himself to destroy such a great machine. He settled for tying it to a tree so it wouldn't be found floating free. That settled, he took a fix on the sun and set out on foot. The 331 ran along the river. Once he found it he would find houses and vehicles.

So far so good. Phil tromped on, the tune of choice humming in his head. Couldn't hum out loud, it might draw attention, but in his head was almost as good. *Soon*, he promised himself, *soon I'll end her life.*

. . . . .

Harvey headed away from Caleb's Cove, making a quick stop to have a word with the officers guarding the bridge. "If we find him on the mainland, I'll let you know. You can return to your usual route after that, unless one of the others needs help here."

That taken care of, he crossed the dirt road behind Whitesand Beach and reached the main road. The 331 had its twists and turns but Harvey pushed as fast as he dared. Although Phil had a head start, he would have to ditch the boat and find transportation once the river ended. However, the man probably had all the skills he needed to make that work.

The 331 merged into King Street, and he turned on the blue and red flashers as he turned right onto Aberdeen Road and headed for the South Shore Regional Hospital. The tension knotting his shoulders eased. He'd be there first. Had to be. And he'd lie in wait for Mr. Phil Doucette.

Only minutes later he was crossing the drive toward the entrance to the emergency department. His phone rang. Dispatch.

He pulled into the curb and turned off the engine. "Conrad here."

"Just thought you'd want to know that a 1995 purple, Ford Ranger was stolen just where King Street turns into the 331."

"How long ago?"

"It's been at least fifteen minutes, maybe longer."

"Thanks." Harvey stepped out of the car and scanned the parking areas. His gaze settled on the Ranger. *Damn it all anyway.* He slammed the door shut and ran to the hospital, burst through the doors and headed for the desk.

"Emily Martin. Where?" He barked out the words.

The nurse pointed and Harvey ran with the nurse trailing after him.

"The third curtain," she called out.

Harvey ripped back the curtain. Phil Doucette stood beside the bed, one hand on the IV tube, a syringe in the other. Only her fingers stuck out from her bandages, but Emily had gripped Phil's shirt sleeve as best she could. She wasn't strong enough to stop him and Phil had managed to stick the needle into the tube.

Harvey grabbed Phil by the scruff of the neck and the arm holding the needle. "Disconnect that tube," he ordered over his shoulder. But the command wasn't necessary. The nurse had already reached across the bed and pulled the IV from Emily's arm. She held up the tube, scanning it.

"One air bubble," she said. "Well above her needle."

Harvey struggled with Phil, knocked the needle out of his hand and pulled his arm behind and up. Phil bent from the waist, spewing curses.

"Ask her where the money is," he demanded. "Ask her who her father was. Ask her. She knows. It was all her fault. He did it because of her."

Harvey managed to get the man turned and headed toward the waiting room. At the edge of the curtained cubicle, he looked back at Emily. "You and I are going to have an honest talk. And no more hedging."

The security guard joined him and they handcuffed Phil to a chair with the guard standing over him. Harvey called for a unit to come and pick up Phil who had settled into muttering curses. Harvey looked at the guard. "You got this? I'll be just a minute away. I want to talk to the victim."

The guard nodded, and Harvey headed back to have that talk with Ms. Emily Martin.

CHAPTER 21

Constable Harvey Conrad stared at the battered woman lying on the bed. Her story was one of the most unusual ones he'd heard in years. When he folded her story into the information he had received on Phil Doucette's crime, it was one twisted tale.

What he'd learned from the police files was that Phil and two friends, Ray and Bobby, had stolen money that was being laundered by the mob. Phil's cousin, Ray Oickle, was killed during the crime. Bobby Jones had disappeared with his five-year-old daughter, after his wife was killed when their car hit a tree. No one knew why the car hit the tree. Phil had gone to jail and while he was there his daughter died of an overdose and his wife ran off with another man.

"So you're telling me that you are that five-year-old girl."

Emily nodded. Her eyes drifted shut and her face grimaced. Although in pain, she'd refused more medications stating she needed to tell Harvey her story with a clear head.

"And you and your father lived under the name Wilson until he thought the mob was catching up with him."

"He didn't say it quite like that, but looking back, I remember he was more afraid of being caught by someone other than the police."

Harvey rubbed his eyes with thumb and forefinger. "When you were almost sixteen, your father got you yet another set of ID. The Emily Martin that you've lived under since?"

Another nod.

He had real trouble with the next part. "And he sent you off on a bus with fifty thousand dollars, in cash, in your knapsack—alone?"

"Yes. He thought if they caught us together, they'd kill us."

"Did you spend that money?"

"Just a bit to get started. When I could, I put back what I'd used and put it all in safety deposit boxes."

"Safety deposit boxes?"

"Well, I couldn't explain to a bank where I got all that cash, could I?"

She was right about that. "And the ID made you eighteen, gave you a driver's license and high school grad papers? Do you realize how farfetched this sounds?"

"Why do you think I never told anyone? He did it so I wouldn't end up in child care somewhere. He had forbidden me to tell anyone for my own safety, and I just got in that mode and stayed there. I know it sounds made up, like from a novel. But not being clear on the dangers, I didn't want to give information to anyone and put them in jeopardy."

He just looked at her. What a far-fetched story. But then, he'd learned over the years that life was often more far-fetched than fiction.

Emily opened her eyes and made contact with his gaze. "I know it sounds weak looking back. But until very recently, it made sense to me. I'd grown up with a fear of police and bad guys stalking me. My father had drilled into me that anyone close to him, or me, could be used as pawns to make him give back the money. And he said, they would kill us even if they got the money."

For now, he had to take her story at face value. "Fair enough. How did you end up here in Caleb's Cove?"

"You know about Phil, right?"

Harvey nodded. He'd gotten very familiar with Phil Doucette in recent hours.

"Well, Dan Grady was the man who got away. Formerly known as Don Wilson. He was someone else before that." She sighed and coughed. "That's the name I wanted, the one before Wilson."

Harvey gave a mental *I knew it.* This was all coming together. "Your father?"

"I hadn't seen him for years, but he contacted me about a month ago."

"How did he know where to find you?"

"We had a system. Anyway, right after I heard from him, I was drugged at a wedding. The next morning, I found mint candies in my clutch purse with a note about the sins of the father. I decided I needed to find my father and get all the information from him. I arrived here. He was here. You know most of the rest."

"Back up a minute. Mint candies?"

"Evergreen lifesavers. Dad loved them."

"But Grady didn't give you the family history you wanted?"

"He said he had most of it in an envelope for me but had more to put in. But then he died."

Voices and clattering broke the quiet. A male voice recited someone's vitals. "She's stable. No broken bones. No injuries. She suffered from the cold and damp in the cave but that's it."

Marta had arrived. Harvey stood and stepped out of Emily's cubicle. He found Lenya in the hallway. "Sounds like she's going to be okay."

Lenya nodded. "Those two boys did a darn good job. They're off getting dry clothing but they'll be along in a bit. That young cop you left took them."

"And Dave Lamont?"

Lenya pointed with her chin. "He's in there with Marta. Hasn't left her side since they transferred her from the rowboat to the stretcher. Seems he's known her a long time."

Lamont knew the storekeeper? How long had he known her? Harvey scratched his chin. What was going on there? "And none of you knew that? I mean, people in Caleb's Cove tend to know everything."

Lenya shrugged and grinned. "The odd thing gets past us, I guess."

Harvey looked at her sideways. He didn't quite buy that. A ruckus out in the waiting room drew his attention and he headed out.

He found Phil struggling to get away. The officer Harvey had sent to the boathouse robbery had arrived and unhooked Phil from the chair.

Harvey grabbed Phil by the back of his collar and pulled him upright. "Calm down. It's over. The only place you're going is back to jail. Kidnapping, attempted murder, murder—you'll be gone a long, long time."

Phil stopped abruptly. "I didn't murder anyone."

"Are you saying that you did not kill Dan Grady aka Don Wilson?"

"Darn right I didn't. I wanted that bastard alive. I wanted him to know that his daughter suffered, like mine did. And I wanted him to know I'd killed her. And for the record the traitor's name was Bobby Jones."

Well, that confirmed the final connection between the two men. The man made a good case for not having killed Grady. But then, his mind seemed a bit warped and his reasoning gruesome. Harvey gestured to the officer. "Take him in. Get him processed. Not up to us to say yay or nay on the murder. Our job is to nail down every scrap of evidence. The rest is up to the jury."

He returned to Emily's cubicle and found Lenya sitting in the chair beside her. Neither woman was saying anything. Just sitting being comfortable together.

Lenya turned and put a finger to her lips. She mimed sleeping and pointed at Emily.

"Not asleep." Emily spoke up.

"I can't stay," Harvey said.

"No worries. I'll keep the child company. No time for anyone to be alone. Not after that nightmare."

Harvey moved to the far side of the bed and put his hand on Emily's shoulder. "You'll be okay now. I just wanted to let you know. I found out your father's real name."

Emily's eyes popped open, her pupils wide and staring. Her mouth opened, closed. She didn't say anything but the look in her eyes did the asking.

"He was Bobby Jones."

"Bobby Jones." Emily whispered the name. "So my mother was Lily Jones." Emily put her good hand over her face, and he realized she was crying. There was a loud sniff, and he gave her a tissue.

Her voice was awed. "My name is Suzie Jones." She whispered, "I am Suzie Jones."

A strangled noise came from Lenya. She was staring at Emily like she'd seen a ghost. "Oh, good Lord," she said. "Oh my."

"Do you know the names?" Harvey asked and Emily turned her head to see Lenya.

"Know their names? Of course I know their names." She laughed through tears. "Lily is my first cousin." She leaned over and kissed Emily on the cheek. "My dear child, we're family." She gripped Emily's hand in hers and smoothed back her hair. "Always did think you looked familiar." She sniffed and reached to the bedside table for a tissue of her own.

Harvey, about to leave, paused and frowned. "You said she *is* your cousin? Don't you mean was your cousin."

Lenya looked down and made a face. "Oh damn. Well, I suppose it's all over now. They're all dead but Phil Doucette."

"And he's in police custody," Harvey said. "Nothing more to fear from him."

Lenya got up and headed out. "I'll be right back."

Emily and Harvey stared after her. What was she up to?

. . . . .

Emily fought back the wave of pain that accompanied her moving. "Wind me up," she said to Harvey. "I want to sit. I want to know what's going on."

Harvey went to the foot of the bed and turned the crank, raising Emily enough for her to see straight ahead.

"That's good." Emily got the words out and let her eyes close. For long seconds she willed the pain to subside.

"Where did Lenya go?" she asked. For her to make such a pronouncement—that they were related. And then to take off? Her fogged brain organized what she knew. If Lenya and Lily were first cousins, then Emily and Lenya were first cousins once removed. Her training let her get that far. *Oh my goodness.* Her heart pounded faster. *I have family here. I belong in Caleb's Cove.* It was almost more than her brain could take in.

She laughed. *Family, family, I have family, I have a home.* Her excitement had her singing in her head.

The curtain to her right swished back and its rollers clattered overhead. Lenya and Dave Lamont stood on the far side of Marta's bed. Like Emily, Marta was propped up and she held Dave's hand. All three of them were crying, but smiling. A chill raced over Emily's skin. *What is going on?*

Marta held out her other hand toward Emily. Dave and Lenya pushed, and Marta's bed came close enough for her to touch Emily's arm. Roaring confusion filled Emily's head and she looked uncomprehendingly at the three of them. She shot a quick look at Harvey and he nodded encouragingly.

"Suzie." Lenya stopped and cleared her throat. "Meet Lily Jones, your mother."

Emily heard the words 'your mother.' The world stopped, her breathing ceased and she blinked. She couldn't have heard correctly.

It couldn't be that easy, to go from being an orphan to having a mother. A real mother. Her mother. In the space of one sentence.

She blinked again and the still-shot moment jumped back into action. *My mother.* She reached for her mother's hand. The contact of skin on skin completed the circuit and emotions like she'd never experienced threatened to explode her heart.

"My baby," Marta murmured. "My Suzie-Q. How I've missed you. I've looked for you all these years. Dave has helped me. He stuck with it even when I'd given up hope. He found Phil and Bobby a few weeks ago. We'd hoped we'd find you. But I was so afraid we wouldn't." She rolled on her side and laid her hand against Emily's cheek. "And here you are."

That vacant spot that had resided in Emily's heart and mind filled to overflowing with a sensation she could barely fathom. *I have a mother. A mother.* She rolled, and stared into Lily's eyes. Tears blurred her vision but she saw the love in her mother's eyes.

Harvey moved in behind her and tucked a pillow along her back.

Lily turned to look at Dave behind her. "Where are my things, the ones from the cave?"

Dave reached into the bedside table and pulled out a bag. He raised an eyebrow at Lily and she nodded. He pulled out a green bundle and handed it over. Lily shook it out.

Emily laughed through her tears. *My frog.*

Lily smoothed the fur and held it out. "I can't believe that you kept it all these years. I gave you this just weeks before…" her voice broke. "You loved it immediately."

Emily let go of her mother's hand with one hand and took the frog and, once again, locked her fingers with her mother's. Connected and not willing to let go. A faint memory of the new frog and her mother's hug sprang to mind.

Behind her, Harvey shuffled and coughed. She glanced at him. *He's crying? Harvey?*

He pulled out a tissue and blew his nose. "I'll leave you with your mother. There's a lot to sort out, but it can wait." And squaring his shoulders, he turned and left.

Lenya patted Marta's shoulder. "Now we can go back to calling you Lily. I'll be in the waiting room for now." She poked Dave. "Come on. Give them some privacy."

Dave leaned over and kissed Lily's cheek. "I'll be here." He turned and followed Lenya out. The curtains closed around mother and daughter.

Emily stared into eyes so much like her own. "I look like you."

"Yes, my darling. You look like I did years ago. The accident changed a lot about me but it didn't stop me loving you."

Emily stroked her mother's face, her fingers tracing the scar down the hairline and chin. "It didn't change a thing. You are still my beautiful Mommy."

Lily rose on one elbow and leaned over and kissed Emily's face. "My dear, dear, daughter, I'll never lose you again."

They were the best words Emily had ever heard.

CHAPTER 22

Harvey stopped outside the cubicle and cleared his throat several times. It would never do to have the troops witness any tears. He had a tough-guy reputation to maintain. But watching that reunion with mother and daughter had triggered unexpected emotions. *I have so much family, I can't imagine living with none.* He cleared his throat again. At least now Emily had her own family.

He headed for the waiting room, followed by Lenya and Dave. They reached the center of the waiting room. Cleaning smells and a faint odor he'd rather not identify filled the room. Harvey turned to Lenya and Dave. "We need to talk."

Dave and Lenya shared a gaze and both nodded.

Lenya reached out and hugged Harvey. "Of course."

Harvey felt his face flush. He didn't usually get hugs. "Let's get out of the middle of the room. Lamont, come, fill me in on the history. Just the high points for now."

Harvey moved away from the desk and into a corner by a silk plant as tall as him. A disembodied voice paged a doctor to the second floor. On the other side of the room a mother and child waited for attention, and an old man in a wheelchair sipped oxygen through a tube attached to a cylinder. Lenya took a seat near Harvey and Lamont. Harvey nodded to Lamont to start.

"The three men, Jones, Doucette and Oickle stole money from an illegal group. It was their drug, prostitution and club money for an entire weekend. The illegal group was led by Doucette's cousin on his mother's side, and Doucette was young enough and stupid enough to think they could grab the money and disappear.

"After taking the money at gunpoint, they ran and later abandoned their car. Jones called his wife, Lily to pick them up. She left her daughter with Phil's wife while she did so. Apparently, when Lily found out what they'd done, she and her husband got into a fight. During the argument, she lost control and drove into a concrete tower holding up an overhead bridge. Oickle and Lily were left for dead." Lamont clutched the back of his head. "But when I arrived at the scene, I found Lily still alive."

Harvey let the information slot into the story-blanks in his head. "How did she end up here under another name?"

"If the men whose money was stolen knew she was alive they'd have watched her in case her husband showed up with the money. The decision was made to post her death notice. She was almost three years in hospital and in rehab. After that, Marta emerged and moved to Caleb's Cove. With her limp and the reconstruction on her face, she was unrecognizable to the locals. Only three local people knew who she was. Her mother, Mrs. Esther Gerber, her cousin, Lenya and Lem Ritcey who arranged for the gravestone."

Harvey shook his head. Laid out point blank like that, it made a great plot for a movie. "And you stuck around?"

Lamont lifted one shoulder and let it drop. "It was my first exposure to such a big case. At first I helped search for her husband and daughter. I visited her and we became friends. She is one gutsy lady. When the case went cold, I kept looking for her daughter. I kept tabs on Phil Doucette for a bit after he was released, but eventually lost track of him. Our luck changed when he showed up in Caleb's Cove. Marta recognized him and let me know. I'm not sure when he realized who she was, but as far as I know, her husband, Dan Grady as you know him, died not knowing she was alive."

The exterior door swished and a whiff of fresh air eddied in the medicinal scent of the emergency department. Turner, Hart and the rookie marched toward Harvey.

He reached out and shook Hart's hand. "Well done." His voice sounded gruff even to him. He kept a firm grip when Hart would have let go. "But if you ever pull a stunt like that again, I'll nail you." He did not specify how he'd nail him. Let the kid think about it.

Hart ducked his head. "I'll try not to."

"Do, not try," Harvey said with a growl. The cocky kid just grinned.

Turner watched the exchange with a smile hovering on his lips. "I must say," he said, "that was one of the best rescues I've ever taken part in. What a rush."

Harvey looked at the ceiling. "Save me from rash young men."

The rookie finally stepped up. "How are they?"

"Good, really good." Harvey told them about the identity and relationship between the two women.

Hart shifted from foot to foot. "Man, that's wild that Emily is really Suzie and she's a cousin to Lenya. Totally rad." He grinned. "Only in Caleb's Cove, eh?"

Harvey narrowed his eyes and stared at Hart. The young man was way too irrepressible. He raised a finger and indicated his fellow officers. "Now, we need to get back to the detachment. I want to go over Grady's autopsy from The Medical Examiner Services. It arrived right after I left to look into this deal. Then it is time to grill Doucette for missing details. And we need to go over everything and figure out who did kill Dan Grady."

Hart saluted the three officers. "I'll stick with Lenya and Dave and get a ride home with them after. Good luck with the investigation."

Harvey started for the door. "Time's a-wasting, boys. Let's get to it. We need to nail down a killer."

. . . . .

Harvey cut across to the Tim Hortons on Lahave Street and picked up a round of coffee and Timbits. The session ahead could be long and arduous. They needed to build their case against Phil Doucette, not only for the kidnapping, but also for the murder of Dan Grady. Pulling together the timeline, the forensic evidence and the witness statements was no easy task. They couldn't afford to miss a detail. And now that the autopsy report was in, he had a whole new pool of information.

He joined the other officers in the bullpen and assigned tasks. "Turner, go through all the witness statements and make a list of what's relevant." He pointed at the rookie, whose name no one seemed to be able to remember. "You, update the timeline on the board along with the appropriate selection of photos." He assigned the task of determining motives to the rookie's partner.

Harvey handed out the coffees and they all settled to their tasks. Back in his office, Harvey read through the autopsy report with growing annoyance. Cause of death was a heart attack and death had been closer to midnight than morning. The manner of death was undetermined. *Undetermined? Well, damn it anyway.* He finished the report and, taking it with him, headed to the bullpen.

"Listen up, boys. Here's what we're faced with. There are two possible scenarios. Either Grady hit his head and had a myocardial infarction or it happened the other way around. He might not have died immediately and there would have been time for the bleeding to occur."

Turner rocked in his chair, hands tucked under his armpits and his head nodding.

Harvey pressed on. "If the head injury came first, someone might have pushed him, and we might have a case for murder or manslaughter." He took a deep breath and looked around at his officers. "But if the heart attack came first, and no one was there, it was decidedly accidental death from normal causes."

Turner stopped rocking. "Someone else was there when he died. We just have to prove it or get a confession."

Harvey nodded. "We do know that whatever did happen, the camper was searched after Grady's death. The searcher is therefore guilty of not reporting the death." He flipped to the report on the fingerprints, the medications and other items collected by the Crime Scene Unit.

"One set of prints and both stray hairs belong to Emily Martin. But she reported the death. Of course, the witness statement from Lamont says she was inside about twenty minutes with the body. She might have searched, looking for the information Grady was supposed to give her."

The rookie tapped a photo on the board and spoke up. "But the mess in the camper looks more like someone angry went through the place."

They continued on through finding Doucette's fingerprint and the subsequent find of his earlier crimes and conviction.

"What we need to know is *when* he was in the camper? You lot nail down as much as you can find, every small detail including Kane Mason's testimony."

He turned to Turner. "Where were the others around midnight?"

"Lamont was by his fire pit and Martin was asleep in her trailer," Turner said. "If there was any reason to suspect them, they don't have alibis. And none of the other campers, other than Lydia Mason, had any connection to Grady or Doucette. And Mason's connection is most likely to Doucette."

Harvey knew what he was implying. There was no reason to suspect an ex-cop and a daughter. "Looks like we're back to the man the Mason kid saw with Grady."

Turner nodded. "The technicians found a hat in the stolen truck that matches Kane's description."

Harvey's hopes rose. "Okay, both Kane and Tammy saw the hat. We'll need to get them to look at it later." He turned to the rookie. "What's on the timeline for us?"

The rookie pointed at the white board. "Lamont heard Grady's door shut around midnight. One other camper told Turner he'd seen the boy 'taking a leak' around midnight. So it was within the window for time of death."

Oh crap. The case might hinge on that camper and a five-year-old boy. Unless they got a confession. He closed the files and signaled Turner to join him. They needed to talk to Doucette.

Turner followed Harvey into the interrogation room. Doucette slouched in the single chair on the far side of the table. Two chairs waited on the opposite side of the table. Harvey and Turner took their seats and opened the files. The still, stale air settled oppressively around them. Turner sat slightly back, leaving Harvey to launch the interview. After delivering all the cautions, Harvey got down to business.

"We know you were in touch with Grady…"

"Bobby-O Jones if you don't mind." Doucette lifted one corner of his mouth in a sneer. "Loser extraordinaire and lying, cheating, deserting…"

Sounds like he has enough hate to kill.

Harvey raised a finger. "Enough. You're here to answer questions and I haven't asked one yet." His low voice brooked no argument.

Doucette sat back. "Whatever."

"Your fingerprint places you in Grady's trailer. You have reason to hate him, and therefore want him dead. It's a given that you will be charged with the kidnapping and attempted murder of two women. All that remains is to determine if you killed Grady." He put a shot of emphasis on the name, defying Doucette's rant. "If you know anything about Grady's death, now is the time to speak up." Harvey sat back and stared at Doucette.

The man pinched his nostrils and sniffed. He slid his butt back in the chair and planted his forearms on the table. "None of this is my fault."

Harvey said nothing. He had two tactics to use. Grilling and listening. Often the latter produced better results.

Doucette looked at each of the officers in turn and then turned his gaze to the video camera up in the corner. He sighed and pulled his gaze back to Harvey. "Look. I know I'm going down for all this shit even if I'm not responsible for most of it. I just want one thing. I want to be sent somewhere out west. If you stick me back in the Quebec system, I'm a dead man. They'll get to me."

Harvey placed one hand flat on the table. "I'll ask," he said. "That's all I can do." He returned to sitting back and staring.

Doucette licked his lips. "Okay then. Like I said, I didn't want him dead. I wanted him alive to know what happened to his daughter." He traced the letter d that some previous suspect had managed to carve in the table top. "If he and that do-gooder wife of his had not fought, the car would never have gone out of control and hit that damn concrete pillar. It's all his fault I was trapped in the car and the police got me. He took off, promising to take care of my family."

Doucette stopped and cleared his throat. "And then he disappeared. It's his fault my wife had to take up with another man, and my Becky turned to drugs." He curled his shoulders and hung his head. He shoulders shook. "He took my wife and daughter." For long moments he sobbed silently.

He appeared to be a beaten man. Harvey coughed. Doucette sat up and wiped his nose on his sleeve.

"He destroyed my family and my life." He turned his head and tipped it as if to spit. At the last moment he obviously thought better of it and turned back to face Harvey.

Once started, the man spewed information like a city water truck spraying dusty streets. Harvey resisted looking at Turner. He did check to make sure the light was still on for the camera and sound recording. The singing of this bird, they wanted on record.

Their silence seemed to let Doucette think he was making good progress. "So you can see, I'm not at fault." He sat straight now, more in control, more cocky. "And then, when I found him here, he had the gall to lie to me." His voice shifted cadence. "*I didn't have all the money* said good old Bobby-O. *It ran out years ago*, he said. *I don't have money to give you.* The lying cheat insisted that was the truth. But it was a lie. I know it was a lie. It had to be. He really ticked me off."

Doucette leaned forward, earnest in his appeal. "So you see, it's not my fault I shoved him. What else could I do? I needed him to own up to the truth. Not my fault he was sick and weak and couldn't stand up against a measly little shove. Not my fault he hit his stupid head. I did check him. If he'd been alive, I'd have left and made an anonymous call to get him help." Doucette sat back. "Remember, I wanted him alive." He shrugged. "But he groaned once and stopped breathing. There was no pulse. So I just left him there."

He shook his head and met Harvey's gaze. "You see how it was, right? And then that sneaky daughter of his had to go and find a way out of the cave. It's her fault I got caught. Her, I'd like to see dead. That was the plan." He started to mumble. "And even that didn't work."

"Please speak clearly." Harvey kept his voice mild.

Doucette banged one fist on the table. "And Bobby-O double crossed me even in death. I couldn't find a damn thing to point me to the money." He sat back and met Harvey's stare. "And that's the damn truth. Take it or leave it." He crossed his arms and clamped his mouth shut.

Harvey slanted a glance at Turner, and in unison, they sat forward, closed their files and rose. Without a word to Doucette they headed for the door. The jailbird's song was done.

The uniformed officer waiting outside opened the door.

"Take him back to the cells," Harvey ordered. "We have what we need."

CHAPTER 23

Emily woke to the sound of a kettle whistling in the kitchen. Joy effervesced under her rib cage and percolated through her, tingling every inch with happiness. She stretched and snuggled in the bed she had slept in as a child. She'd been four the last time she'd visited her grandmother and, although she didn't remember, her mother and grandmother did. The past weeks had been filled with old stories and pictures and gradually, those forgotten years had come to life. Now she was staying with her grandmother, the one with all the frogs in her closed-in front veranda. *Family is even better than I imagined.*

"Suzie, your coffee is ready." Grandmother Gerber's voice floated up the stairs. She'd gone and bought her first-ever coffee maker just for Emily.

Suzie? Emily? Who am I? The legalities and processes for changing all her records from Emily Martin to Suzie Jones were astronomical. Not to mention the records in Suzie Wilson's name. Paper work was far more complicated than deciding on a name to be called. She stretched once more and got out of bed. For the moment, she answered to both Suzie and Emily. *I need a good lawyer to sort it all out.*

"Good morning, Grandma." The thrill surged through her again. She accepted her cup of coffee and settled at the table by the window. Breakfast would appear soon. Her grandmother insisted on preparing one for her, and how could she turn down homemade soda biscuits and eggs?

The tapping of the cane on the stairs announced her mother's coming. Everyone had sorted out her name. They called her Marta Lily and it suited her. But Emily didn't think she could take to Emily Sue.

Marta Lily joined them in the kitchen. "Good morning, sweetheart." She kissed Emily on top of the head and joined her at the table.

She leaned over and planted a matching kiss on her mother's cheek. "Morning, Mom."

Emily looked around the table. Three generations of women all together in a country kitchen. She laughed from the sheer pleasure of it. The love and comfort of family and home was marvelous.

I'm sure it helped me heal. And today, I'm going shopping with my mother to buy a dress for the party tonight. Such an ordinary occurrence for most daughters. For her, it was a priceless gift.

Just before suppertime, Emily walked with her mother and grandmother across the café parking lot. The evening's gala included a meal. *And here we are, the three generations of women, dressed to the nines and ready to party until midnight. Just like three Cinderellas.* Emily laughed and took her grandmother's hand on one side and tucked her free hand gently under her mother's elbow on the other.

An edge of sorrow tried to intrude. It would have been wonderful if her father had lived to see them all together, but he'd spent a lot of money on changing identities and eventually buying a house. That was one thing Phil got right. Bobby Jones had had the money, much of it in offshore accounts.

The police had tracked down his permanent address by showing his photo around the cancer clinics. They'd visited his house and talked to neighbors and learned more. The best information came in an unexpected way. When Lenya had retrieved Emily's climbing gear, one rope was stuck. She pulled hard and it dislodged an envelope wedged into the top of the storage cubbyhole. The documents, deeds, and banking records in the package laid out the entire fortune.

Emily sighed. She wanted no part of the illegal proceeds that had resulted in two men dead and a family torn apart. Turning that entire package, including the fifty thousand dollars from her safety deposit boxes, over to Harvey had lifted the last of her worries.

Harvey Conrad. Emily liked him. He stopped by to see how she and Marta Lily were making out. He told them it was for Mrs. G's cookies. Her heart did a flip. It might be more. She'd wait and see what happened. She followed her Grandmother's slow walk to the café.

Harvey, looking handsome in a buttoned-up shirt and cargo pants, was waiting by the café. He smiled at her and opened the door. As she passed, he stroked her shoulder, his touch warm and reassuring.

The women stepped into view past the counter, and the room rocked with clapping and cheers. Emily stood with an arm around her mother and grandmother and let the tears run down her cheeks unchecked. The warmth wrapped around her. *I didn't know acceptance could feel like this.*

She looked around at the smiling faces. Her cousins, Lenya and Gwen, were front and center with Hart right beside them. In the middle she saw Devon and her husband, Greg, plus Kelsey with her husband, Sam. Adam and Kane hopped up and down in excitement. And to the right of the crowd, she saw two faces she hadn't expected. Mandy and Sandra, all the way from Northern Ontario, stood there grinning from ear to ear.

Family, new friends, old friends. Emily turned and kissed her mother's cheek and then hugged her grandmother before heading into the crowd waiting to greet her. Contentment washed over her. *Life can't get any better than this.*

About the Author

Write what you want to read.

An avid reader from elementary school on, Mahrie often read twelve books a week. Once she'd read the Nancy Drew books, mysteries dominated her lists. Agatha Christie, Dick Frances and Dorothy Gilman, among many others, set the tone for her reading and writing.

Over the years she's published articles, poems and short stories. She has belonged to writing groups and attended conferences and workshops and, in later years, taught in all these areas. Her stories involve ordinary people who get caught up in extraordinary situations that push them to be more, and do more, than they ever thought possible.

Mahrie is a member of Alberta Romance Writers' Association and a graduate of Calgary's Citizen's Police Academy and Private Investigation 101. She lives north of Calgary, Alberta with her hubby and a cat called Kotah.

www.mahriegreid.com

www.facebook.com/mahriegreid

Other books by Mahrie

Caleb Cove Mysteries, Book 1

Came Home Dead

Be careful what you do in life for your past may come back to haunt you.

When a corpse surfaces in the aftermath of a hurricane, the storm has only begun for Devon Ritcey. Friends and family in Caleb's Cove offer up an excess of secrets and suspects. And her big secret can make her a suspect. Can she work with ex-cop, ex-lover, Greg Cunningham to uncover the killer and keep the island's inhabitants safe while guarding her own secrets?

Caleb Cove Mysteries, Book 2

Came Home to a Killing

All of our lives may be an illusion.

When Kelsey Maxwell learns her life is lie, she's determined to uncover the truth. She doesn't expect her quest to lead to fraud, murder, and a killer with a knife. Working with Sam Logan, a security consultant, she follows her father's trail chased by criminals who want the evidence he's stolen. Caught in a race for the prize, Kelsey doesn't know if the truth will set her free, or get them all killed.

Made in the USA
Charleston, SC
07 March 2017